RESCUE DOGS

JET

RESCUE DOGS

JET

JANE B. MASON
AND SARAH HINES STEPHENS

Scholastic Inc.

This book is a work of fiction. Names, characters, places, and incidents are either the product of the author's imagination or are used fictitiously, and any resemblance to actual persons, living or dead, business establishments, events, or locales is entirely coincidental.

ISBN 978-1-338-36210-7

10 9 8 7 6 5 4 3 2 1   20 21 22 23 24

Printed in the U.S.A. 40
First printing 2020

Book design by Stephanie Yang

For the people who work tirelessly to care
for dogs who have been abandoned,
neglected, mistreated, or misunderstood

01

The black-and-white border collie pup dozed in a dirt patch, his feet twitching. He dreamed of running. Fast, with no collar. He dreamed of chasing butterflies. He dreamed of eating until his belly felt full. Then, all of a sudden, he was jolted awake. In the dim light he saw the short leash and the stake holding him hostage in the dusty yard. He heard an awful grumbling noise, and it wasn't his empty stomach. It was deeper and darker and coming from everywhere at once. No. Not everywhere. It was coming from the sky far away. He raised his nose and sniffed the air. He smelled something like metal. Or electricity. He heard the distant rumble again.

The pup sat up, alarmed. He had never heard this noise before. It wasn't a car or an animal. The sky was darker than usual. And the air felt heavier and wetter with each passing moment. The air felt like he could lick it.

A flash of light startled the dog, and he began to pace as a large wet drop landed on his black-furred head. He shook it off and walked one way and the other and then one way again. He barked, afraid. Whatever this was, it was scary. No, it was terrifying!

The drops started to fall faster, and soon the dog could feel them seeping through his fur to his skin underneath. He trembled and whined. He chewed at the tether holding him to the exposed spot in the yard, even though he knew it was useless.

A few minutes later the back door to the house swung open and a boy appeared. His shoulders were hunched against the water coming from the sky, and he ran the few steps to the center of the yard and squatted down.

"It's okay, Mutt." The boy unclipped the tether from the pup's collar. The sky boomed again and the pup shook. The boy scooped him into his arms. "Shhhh," he whispered, wrapping him in an old towel that smelled like mice and stagnant water. "You're coming with me."

As the boy carried him toward the back steps, the dog looked around nervously. He'd never been in the house. He wasn't *allowed* in the house. He huffed, blowing out air to get the bad smell of the towel out of his nose.

Awkwardly the boy grasped the door handle, tugged open the door, and stepped inside. The dog squinted in the harsh brightness coming from the light bulb that dangled from the ceiling. His white-furred nose sniffed the air. He'd spent days longing to be unclipped from the leash that held him captive in the yard, but now that he was inside he thought outside might be better . . . at least when the sky was not growling and spitting. The house was dark. It smelled like something that made the pup squirm. Something scarier than a storm. This was where the mom lived. And the mom yelled. A lot. The hair on the pup's back stood at attention.

"What do you think you're doing with that in here?" The dark shadow of the boy's mother suddenly loomed in the kitchen, yelling. The puppy felt a shiver go through the boy as the sky boomed again and the boy pulled the puppy closer, squeezing the air out of the small dog's lungs.

"I wanted to get him out of the rain," the boy answered quietly.

The mom threw back her head, howling. "He's a mangy dog! Probably has fleas and who knows what else! I never should have let you talk me into bringing him home in the first place. Take him back outside and tie him up. He'll get a bath out of it."

The boy knew better than to argue. Arguing only made his mom angrier, and that never ended well. So he took the puppy back outside, thumping down the three steps into the now muddy yard. He stopped at the bottom of the stairs and looked around.

"I'm not going to tie you up again," he said secretively as a jagged light flashed in the sky.

The pup tried not to shake but couldn't help it.

He trembled all over as the boy set him down beside the wall of the house.

"You can curl up under here," the boy said. He put the smelly towel underneath a table missing two legs, which was propped up against the wall. The little pup's black ears flopped forward. He didn't know exactly what the boy was saying, but he was speaking softly. The dog liked that. And the area where he'd placed the towel was protected from the wet drips.

"It's like a fort!" the boy whispered, sounding excited. He got down on all fours and started to crawl in with the dog. "Move over, Mutt," he said. "I'm coming in, too!"

Then a voice, louder than the thunder, roared through the screen door. The mom had been watching. "I said tie him up and get back in here!" The dog heard a foot stomp and angry mumbling. "Last thing I need is you catching your death in a storm and slapping us with doctor bills on top of everything else."

The dog heard the boy sigh and saw the air go

out of him. The boy backed out of the den he'd made.

"Well? Go on. Tie him up and get in here!" the mom shouted again.

The boy wiped his nose on his sleeve. "Come on, Mutt." He pulled the small dog out of the fort and carried him back to where he'd been in the first place, fastening him to the stake in the ground. "You probably don't care about the stupid storm, anyway," he whispered. His face was wet, a mix of tears and raindrops.

The pup lay down, shaking. He put his head on his paws and felt the drops fall harder and faster. He felt something else, too. Something that tugged on his insides. It wasn't just fear. It was something lonely. It was knowing that he was not a part of this pack—the human pack that lived in the house and kept him out. They'd brought him home, but the person in charge didn't want him. And she never would.

02

Mutt—that's what the boy called him—took a long sniff of the hard, dry dirt that surrounded him. It smelled the same as it had the day before, and the day before that. Still he huffed and snuffled until he was certain he had smelled every millimeter that he could reach. He hoped to find an ant or some other creepy-crawly that he could eat or play with, if only for a moment. But there was no sign of life in the circle of dusty earth other than the puppy himself. Every blade of grass that once grew underneath him had been gone for months, as were any living creatures.

The puppy's stomach growled. He longed for food and water. He licked the ground and then his nose, his parched pink tongue reaching up to touch his cracked snout. Licking his nose only made it hurt more. It only made him thirstier.

He nudged his water bowl hopefully. The dusty dish moved across the ground with a noisy scrape. It was upside down and empty—he had accidentally stepped in it while circling the stake. He hoped the sound of it moving now would bring the boy out of the house, because he didn't dare bark. Barking would bring the *mom* out of the house. That was something he tried to avoid at all costs.

The border collie mix was black and white and a little brown from the bald patch of earth he'd spent every day on since he'd arrived—tied in the center of the run-down yard. The rope attached to his collar allowed him to move a few feet in any direction, but that was all. He could not reach the back steps to the house, or the little patch of weeds that looked nice for chewing, or the sad-looking tree next to the fence that offered a tiny pool of shade.

Sometimes he dreamed of burrowing under one of the pieces of rubbish—mostly cast-off furniture and car parts—that lay scattered across the yard. But he could not reach those, either. The collar around his neck had grown tight since his arrival. His fur was wearing off beneath it . . . rubbed bald in patches. When he tried to yank away from the rope, the plastic choker just bit painfully into the hairless spots until they were raw.

The skinny puppy lay down, feeling defeated. Dust rose around him as he heaved a long sigh. He closed his eyes, letting images swim in his head. He felt longings deep in his fuzzy chest. He longed for softness, for coolness, for comfort. Hazy memories flickered in his mind like distant sounds and scents . . . memories of a life before this one. Memories of wriggling bodies—his brothers and sisters—all snuggled up against him. Memories of the sleepy pleasure of a belly full of warm milk. Memories of his mother's soothing tongue, wet and warm, on the top of his head. That was all he knew until the moment he was wrenched away from his mama and dropped into a box with his litter-mates. The pup twitched in his sleep, remembering the feeling of being dangled in the air, the barks of his confused brothers and sisters, and then his own desperate yelps mixed in, too. They all wanted to go back to their cozy den! They all wanted to be close to their mama!

The pup twitched again, recalling the bangs of slamming doors and the growl of a car engine. The brief, scary journey in the rattling car had lasted long enough to make the puppy's milky meal slosh around in his tummy. Then the ride was over. He and his siblings were pulled from the hatchback and plunked onto a sidewalk. They waited with the person who smelled like home, but not for long. People stood over them. Voices sounded over their heads. The new people surrounding them smelled strange. Different. The puppy was curious. He pawed at the side of the cardboard box and craned his neck to see more.

"Look at that one! It's got two different colored eyes!" a voice, higher pitched than the others, called. A small hand reached down and grabbed him a little too tightly.

For a moment the puppy was squashed against a young boy's chest. The boy smelled of earwax and chewing gum and food from a can. Someone put something all the way around his neck and clipped something else onto it. A collar and a leash. Then he was plopped onto the rough pavement. He shook to get the collar off, but it stayed put. The boy jerked the leash. The collar squeezed around his throat every time the leash was pulled. And the chewing-gum boy liked pulling.

The boy tugged the puppy across a large expanse of hot pavement, away from his brothers and sisters. He yelped back to them, but the boy didn't understand. He just kept pulling. Then he picked up the puppy and loaded him into another car. This one had cracked seats and made more noise than the first one. The woman who drove smelled like smoke and growled a lot. This ride was long. It went on and on, and the dog's belly flipped and flopped. Then, all of a sudden, his mouth filled with warm, slippery saliva and his stomach turned inside out, sending its milky contents all over the back seat.

"What the . . . !" the mom yelled. "I told you this was a bad idea! You're going to clean every bit of that up! And don't think for one second that animal will be allowed in the house!"

The house. That was where the boy and his mom lived. The dog had only seen the inside twice. Once, on that first day when he'd been pulled from the front door to the back, and then for a few minutes during the thunderstorm.

"You'll stay here," the boy had told him quietly while his mother used a hammer to pound a large rusty stake into the center of the yard. When she finished pounding she'd attached the leash to the stake. "Stay," she'd barked at him. As if he'd had another choice.

The mom made the little dog cower. He pressed his belly to the ground and flattened his ears whenever he heard her coming. Luckily he didn't see her much. As long as he didn't bark, she almost always stayed inside.

At first the boy came out to sit with him a lot. It made the pup happy to hear the screen door bang.

The boy brought food and water. He liked to hold the pup and rub behind his ears. The boy would stay with him until the yelling started inside the house. Then he'd set the little pup back down in his dusty circle.

"You're lucky you live out here, Mutt," he'd tell him, though the pup didn't know what "lucky" meant.

🐾 🐾 🐾

The sound of yelling and the bang of the porch door woke the dog. He jumped to his feet and shook off the dirt. He wagged and wagged at the sight of the boy. He wagged so hard he practically wagged himself over! The boy was the dog's only company and only source of food. He sniffed the air to see if he'd brought him any scraps. Once or twice the boy had smuggled out a bit of dinner for him. But today he just sat down outside the pup's reach with a bowl of something that smelled cheesy and delicious. The small dog stared; his drool dripped onto the dirt. He strained against his collar to try to reach any morsels that might fall. The boy ignored him as he dipped his spoon into his bowl of creaminess.

After he had taken several bites the boy scooched a tiny bit closer, but still out of the pup's reach. "Are you hungry, Mutt?" He dipped his spoon into the bowl again, watching the drooling dog as he slid the mouthful past his own lips.

The pup sat, transfixed and hopeful.

The boy narrowed his eyes and took another bite. He made a big show of swallowing. "Mmmmmm. It's delicious," he said.

A whimper escaped the pup's throat. His stomach grumbled. The boy's eyes narrowed even more. He dropped the spoon into the bowl.

"You want to lick it?" he asked in a softer voice, and stepped closer. But just then the back door slammed and the mom started in their direction. "Get in here and clean up your mess, Howie!" she yelled. The boy's eyes flitted in her direction as he leaped to his feet. "Coming!" he called. "I'll be back with your dinner later, Mutt," he added in a whisper.

But there was a lot of yelling that night, and the

boy did not return with dinner. When he finally came the next day he brought a small bowl of kibble and filled the water bowl. While the pup ate, the boy tinkered with the smelly old refrigerator in the yard. "Gross!" he said, pulling rancid fast food from a bag. He crumpled the paper and tossed it aside.

The quick movement caught the border collie's attention. The bag was close enough to reach! He pounced, catching the crumpled wrapper between his paws before jumping back. The trash ball skittered away and he gleefully went after it again, ears and tail flying high.

"You like to play chase, Mutt?" the boy asked. The pup let out a bark in reply. Yes, he did!

"How about this?" The boy picked up a small stick and shook it. The pup leaped into the air as the boy tossed it. He ran a few short steps, grabbed the stick in his teeth, and brought it back. The boy smiled and threw the stick again. And again, and again. The pup barked happily, and the boy laughed. They were both having fun! They were playing together!

The pup was so focused on the stick he barely heard the sound of the mom's car pulling into the driveway. He barked at the boy to tell him to throw it. The boy was looking over the fence, though. He heard the engine turn off. He threw the stick, but too far. The pup sprinted after it. When he reached the end of his tether it yanked him back and cut into his neck. He let out a yelp.

The boy turned to the pup. His shoulders tight, he walked over and picked up the stick. He threw it again, angrily and out of the pup's reach.

The pup went after it again. He was almost there when YANK! The collar bit into him so sharply he fell onto the dirt.

This time the boy laughed. It wasn't a happy laugh like before, though. This laugh sounded mean. It sent the pup's tail between his legs and flattened his ears.

"Stupid Mutt," the boy snickered. He threw the stick once more. Though the pup tried to remember that he couldn't run outside his tethered circle, the whizzing object got the better of him. There was something inside him that insisted he get it, get it, *get it*!

The dog was stopped short again with a cry.

The noise must have caught the mom's attention. "What are you doing out here!" she yelled over the fence. "I told you to start dinner!"

The boy looked at the ground, then at his dog. His eyes narrowed. He kicked the dirt and threw the stick so far it flew over the fence. The pup let out a whimper. "Shut up, Mutt. You don't know anything," the boy grumbled, and stomped into the house.

After that the pup didn't see the boy for a long time. When he finally did come back, he did not throw a stick. He did not fill the water bowl. He poured half a cup of dusty kibble into the water bowl instead. "That's all we have," he said in a low voice. He didn't laugh or smile or even look at the dog with his beady eyes. He just dumped the food and walked slowly back into the house and let the door close behind him with a bang.

The puppy stifled a whine. He wished he could

chew through the tether and run around the yard. He wished he could chase flying sticks without getting choked. He wished he could find his warm mama and snuggly siblings. He wished he could reach a patch of shade.

He wished he had never been brought here.

03

Days passed slowly for the tied-up dog, but nights were a little better. They were cooler, and the mom didn't shout—she only snored. There were other creatures out at night, too. He could smell the shy possums slowly passing, though they always kept their distance. He smelled the curious rats that ventured closer, hoping he had left a bit of kibble. And sometimes cats and fat raccoons slinked past. The pup was comforted by these night creatures and wished they would stay, but they never did.

One morning after a restless night of too many noises, the dog opened his eyes and knew that something was different. There was a heavy silence.

He didn't hear stomping feet or mumbling voices or clanking dishes. He lifted his nose. He didn't smell bitter coffee, or burnt toast, or souring milk. It was quiet. So quiet.

Too quiet.

It was only quiet in the house at night, or when the mom and the boy were away. It was never quiet in the morning. The pup thought they must have left early. He stood up, stretched, and shook himself off, jangling his collar. He walked the three steps to his dishes. His food bowl was empty—the boy hadn't thought to feed him before he left. He lapped up some stale water. When the sun hit it, it would warm quickly and soon be filled with floating bugs. But for now it was cool from the night air.

Making his way around the circle of packed earth, the dog saw a stick too far away to reach. He picked up a small splinter of wood and chewed it until it was too tiny to catch between his teeth. He circled again. There was nothing to do but wait, so he lay back down, rested his chin on his white-tipped paws, and blew his breath out through his nose.

From his spot in the center of the yard, the dog heard and smelled the whole day pass. He smelled the engines of cars as people headed to work and school. He heard the shouts of children boarding a school bus. He tried to ignore the squirrels that ran along the top of the fence . . . their own personal highway that took them from backyard tree to backyard tree. They only taunted and laughed at him, anyway. He tracked the sound of the mail carrier making her way up and down the street. The sound of her footsteps, the shuffle of paper, the thump of the mailboxes closing. He'd never seen the mail carrier. He didn't know exactly what she was doing when she stopped by each house, but the sounds she made were familiar. He knew the rhythm of her footfalls, and recognized her humming . . .

Hours passed and the children returned to the neighborhood, but not the boy. Not today. Then the cars came back, but not the mom's car with its strange, smelly engine.

The dog's stomach complained. Still, he did not worry. It wasn't the first time he'd gone a whole day without food. He let the cooling air of the evening comfort him. Tomorrow there would be kibble.

The next morning the silence was heavier still. The dog stretched toward the steps. Not even a creak came from the house. He whined, just a little. The door remained shut.

The day passed.

Then another.

And another.

Each day the weather grew hotter and the dog hungrier. He didn't have the energy to walk his circle in the heat wave with an empty belly. He just lay there, panting in the sun. His water was long gone. His nose was drier than dust. Lying on his side, he heard the neighborhood going through its motions. The mail carrier didn't hum, and her steps were slower in the heat. The squirrels stopped taunting him. Maybe they thought he was dead.

It was hard to sleep with his hungry stomach twisted up tight. The little dog was afraid, and not the way he was afraid of the mom yelling. He was afraid he would never go anywhere else—never see or smell or taste or feel anything but the punishing heat and gnawing hunger, the choking thirst and the awful loneliness.

The fear made him muster all his strength and pull hard on the rope holding him. He pulled and chewed. He reared. He jerked his head back and forth. His collar tightened around his raw, rubbed neck. He barely felt it. It was nothing compared to his hunger.

The pup knew he had to get away. There was nothing for him in the deserted backyard. Even the shouting mom would be welcome now. So he did the only thing he could do. The thing he was trained *not* to do. He barked. He barked and barked and barked. He barked until his throat felt like it would crack.

But nobody heard him.

And nobody came.

Another day passed. The little dog's body was weak and shrinking. His bones hurt where they touched the ground. His mind was swimmy. He wished it would rain. He longed for the drops of water that fell from the sky, even if it meant he would hear its terrible boom. He longed for a cloud to make a minute of shade. He tried to dig down to cooler dirt. His paws scratched uselessly on the hard-packed clay. He didn't have the strength. He lay back down, his white muzzle and paws stained red.

Stretching his neck, the pup chewed the itchy fur on his haunches until he had bald spots on his legs to match the hairless patches on his neck. His eyes grew heavy and dull. It was hard to see clearly. He staggered to the dry water bowl and pawed at it. He lifted his head to howl, but his throat was too parched to make a sound. His breathing was shallow under the heat of the sun. His head hung low, and he lay down. So. Tired. He felt dizzy just lying there. Lowering his head to his paws, he closed his eyes to the world . . .

04

Aiden Shook pulled into the empty driveway of the run-down house on Farallon Avenue and cut the engine of his Toyota. Leaning forward on the steering wheel of the truck, he peeked at the house through his windshield and exhaled a slow sigh. It was a sad sight. The small house had been in need of repair for years, but the last winter had really done it in. Aiden scratched behind his ear and chewed on his bottom lip as he took in the extent of it. The paint was peeling off in large curls. One of the windows was broken, and another two cracked and held together with duct tape. The front screen door hung on a single hinge. He sighed again. There was sure to be more damage and disarray inside.

Climbing out of the driver's seat, Aiden knew that once again his wife, Ruby, was right—the house had been deserted. Aiden worked for the county. It was his job to investigate potentially abandoned houses and make sure they didn't turn into squats, with people living in them illegally, or worse, plain hazards. Ruby, who was a mail carrier, helped him out. She and her coworkers were often the first to know when a house became empty—the mail started to pile up, and nobody was ever home. If they spotted the signs, Ruby made sure to update Aiden on the uncollected mail over breakfast. Just that morning she'd let him know about the old place on Farallon. Aiden could have predicted this one would go empty. Anyone in town could have seen this coming. Elise Collins and her boy, Howie, had been on a sinking ship from the moment Ron Collins passed the year before. There had been lifelines thrown their way, but Elise was too angry and too sad to try to catch them. She was too angry and sad to show up at work, too. The grocery store had no choice but to let her go. After that, anyone paying attention knew it was only a matter of time before she lost the house.

The front step creaked under Aiden's weight. He gingerly opened the screen, knocked, and waited. After a moment he knocked again. "Hello?" he hollered. He wasn't expecting an answer unless scavengers or kids were exploring inside. After a solid five minutes of knocking—it was important to be cautious when investigating alleged abandoned homes—he tried the handle and found it unlocked. "Hello?" he called again as he stepped inside. He paused, letting his eyes adjust to the dim light.

Out in the yard, the pup stirred. He thought he heard something. Shouts? Footsteps? The front door? He lifted his head, but a wave of dizziness made him lay it back down. It was probably nothing. He'd been having dreams . . . dreams about people returning. In them he saw the boy carrying bags of food. He saw him turning on the bubbling hose. When he opened his eyes it all disappeared . . .

the boy, the food, the water. So he kept them closed and tried not to think about how hot and tired and thirsty he felt.

Aiden mopped his brow with the bandanna he kept stuffed in his back pocket. He was tempted to tie it over his nose and mouth to ward off the awful smells inside. The house reeked of mildew and rotting garbage. Elise hadn't bothered to clean on her way out, which wasn't surprising. People abandoning their homes rarely did. And the heat wave was speeding up the decay. Aiden coughed and rummaged around in the kitchen until he found a big trash bag. He'd clear out the worst offenders before sealing the house.

The electricity was off and the food in the fridge had spoiled. He quickly cleared the sticky shelves: a milk carton (mostly empty), expired condiments, and a head of lettuce turning to a slimy dark liquid in the crisper. He left the refrigerator door propped open and held the bag closed with his fist before moving to the other rooms. Some of the furniture was gone, but some of it had been left behind—much of it broken, all of it worn. Even in the gloomy light coming through closed curtains he could see the walls were stained and peeling. He peeked out the back door and sighed at the overgrown weeds along the fence and the jumble of junk scattered all over the yard.

The city would need to send out a hauler, a good cleaning crew, and an inspector to see whether the house could be made structurally safe. It was entirely possible they'd need to tear it down. They couldn't just let it turn into a pile of trash—a dilapidated house left to rot could really bring down a neighborhood in addition to creating a liability for the county.

After taking a last look around, Aiden headed back outside. He was happy to breathe the fresh air, even if it was ninety-five degrees. He slung the trash bag into the back of his pickup and pulled out the dinged-up red toolbox that always traveled with him. Back on the porch, he pulled out his drill. Working swiftly, he installed a latch, drilling four quick holes and sending long screws deep into the wood to secure it to the door and frame. When he was finished, he slid a padlock through the loop to keep out intruders.

The whirring whine of the drill made the dog in the backyard lift his head again. It throbbed, but this time he fought the wave of dizziness. Something told him the sounds were real. There was someone here. At the house. A lone cloud crossing the faded blue sky passed in front of the sun. The seconds-long reprieve from the relentless heat provided a moment of clarity, and suddenly the dog was sure. Yes. He heard bootsteps!

"Wuhh!" He tried to bark, but almost nothing came out. "Wuhf!" he tried again. And again. "Wuarf!" he barked out at last. He swallowed hard and barked again, louder. "Warf! Arf! Arf!"

With the lock latched Aiden picked up the spare screws and put them with his tools. He slipped the battery pack off his drill and laid it on top before latching the metal box. He started back to his car, hesitating when he reached the driveway. Did he just hear a . . . *bark*? The noise he'd heard was faint, and not quite right. And Ruby, who was very aware of all the dogs in the neighborhood, hadn't said anything about the Collins boy having a pet. But there it was again. It sounded as though it was coming from the backyard.

Scratching his head, Aiden walked quickly to the wooden side gate and tugged it open, nearly toppling the fence. He scanned the jumble of discarded junk running down the side of the house. He almost turned back—there was no way there could be anything alive in this dump—but then heard it again. A hoarse bark, almost like a whisper. When he rounded the corner of the house Aiden nearly jumped out of his skin. It was easy to see why he'd missed it before, but it was a good thing he'd come back. There, lying in a worn patch of dirt, was a dust-covered black-and-white dog. Less than a year old, judging by the size.

Aiden approached, his green eyes filled with alarm. The pup was breathing, but clearly emaciated and barely alive. The choke collar around his neck had broken the skin, and his body was covered in scabs and dirt. Aiden could count every one of the poor critter's ribs through what was left of his fur. He stooped, then knelt down. "Hey there," Aiden said, gently placing a hand on the pup's body. The dog let out a tiny whimper in response. He attempted a wag of his tail. It twitched, but he didn't have the strength to lift it. Barking had taken the last of his energy out of him.

Aiden gulped. "What have they done to you?" He was half-afraid to move the poor creature . . . He didn't want to cause any additional damage. The dog was in terrible shape as it was.

The pup tried to lift his head to see the person crouched beside him, but couldn't. This person wasn't the boy. Or the mother. He was a stranger. The dog should have been afraid, but he felt nothing. He was barely aware of his collar being loosened around his neck. Barely aware of something underneath him. As his body was lifted, an intense haziness overtook everything. His eyes closed and the little dog's world went dark.

05

Aiden struggled not to speed as he made his way through town to the Midland Animal Rescue, or MA Rescue, on the corner of McArthur and Ninth. The tiny pup lay wrapped in an old blanket Aiden kept in the truck. He wasn't moving. "Hold on, buddy," Aiden told the dog. "We're almost there."

The emaciated border collie didn't respond, and the county worker prayed he was still alive while he tried to focus on the road. After what seemed like an eternity, he pulled into the MA Rescue lot and found a parking place near the front of the building. He opened the passenger door and picked up the dog as gently as he could, taking care not to jostle him any more than was necessary. He was so thin it seemed like he might break.

Inside, the lobby was nearly empty, which Aiden knew was lucky—he'd seen it crammed with people and animals on more than one occasion. The woman behind the front desk, Jessica, took one look at the man and the bundle in his arms and made an intercom call to the folks in the back. "I need a tech to the lobby, stat," she said.

Within seconds a young man in blue scrubs appeared at Aiden's side. He didn't have to ask anything—Aiden just started talking. "I found him tied up in the backyard of an abandoned house. No idea when his people left him, or how long he was there."

"Far too long," the vet tech, whose name tag read LIAM, said. His expression was grim. "People can be so cruel," he added. He reached out his arms, and the two men made the transfer as gently as they could. The pup weighed almost nothing, but his eyes flickered as Liam settled him in his arms. "Well, he's somewhat conscious. That's good," he said. Cradling the dog, Liam disappeared down the hall and into exam room four.

Aiden's arms felt surprisingly empty and his gaze held on the door to the exam room. He watched a vet knock lightly and enter after the pup and the tech. He jolted a bit when the door closed firmly behind her, feeling relief and worry wash over him at the same time.

"If you leave your name and number, we'll update you," Jessica said, her voice startling him a second time.

Aiden stepped forward and she handed him a pen and paper. While he was writing, she tried to reassure him. "Dr. Wells is excellent. She has a lot of experience with strays and abandoneds."

Abandoneds. The word echoed in Aiden's head. He'd never heard "abandon" used as a noun before. As he handed back the pen and turned to leave, another word leaped into his head: "tortureds." He hoped Dr. Wells was excellent with those as well.

Behind the door of exam room four, the

black-and-white dog lay on a cool metal table while two big people leaned over him. Even in his semi-conscious state the dog could tell that he was inside a building—like the house, but also nothing like the house. It smelled strong, but not bad. Not rotten or old or dirty. The surface underneath him felt hard against his protruding bones—harder even than the patch of dirt he'd been lying on forever, but at least there was no sun in here. And, mercifully, the choking collar was gone.

"You poor thing," Dr. Wells murmured, leaning down to see how deep the young dog's breathing was. Or rather, how shallow. "It's all right—we're going to help you."

She completed a quick exam, touching him with expert lightness, while Liam stroked the dog's head, noting his bald patches and dirty, matted fur. "People can really suck," he said.

Dr. Wells nodded. "They can. It's hard when you don't know what the story is—what happened. His dehydration and malnourishment are pretty severe—we'll need to work slowly and methodically so we don't overwhelm his system. It's going to be touch-and-go for a good while."

"A slow drip of IV fluids, then?" Liam asked.

Dr. Wells nodded. "The slowest possible."

The puppy's eyes flittered. He was too far gone to pay attention to the people or conversation going on above him, though some tiny part of him was curious. He just didn't have any energy to feed his curiosity. It seemed as if he were in a looong, echoing tunnel. Were those the vet's hands examining his body? He wasn't sure. Was that a poke on his leg? He wasn't sure about that, either. He thought he heard a faraway rustling sound. He thought something was being wrapped around one of his legs. Was it the same leg? He couldn't tell.

The puppy tried to breathe through his sunburned nose. He tried to stay calm. Besides the good moments with the boy, humans had only been cruel to him. The only safety he'd known was with his mama and siblings, and he had been taken from them so long ago. Humans were not to be trusted. And yet, it was a human that picked him up out of the dust. A human that brought him here. And now the people helping him were human, too.

It was confusing. It was too much to think about. It was almost too much to lie here. The puppy went back to just trying to breathe.

The IV drip began doing its work, moving fluid, drop by tiny drop, into the pup's body. Liam tapped the line to make sure there were no air bubbles. "Do you think he'll make it?" he asked Dr. Wells quietly.

The vet glanced down at the wisp of a dog, her eyes equally sad and worried. "Hard to say," she replied honestly. She stroked the border collie's mangy fur, then went to the cupboard to get a washcloth to try and clean him up a bit so she could get some antibiotic ointment onto his countless sores. She came back to the exam table and looked down at the pup's face. "We don't know anything about his personality. If he's a fighter, then possibly yes. But it's pretty much up to him."

The pup had no idea what they were saying, but somehow understood that they were talking about him. He opened his eyes and tried to see the people clearly. It took a little while and a lot of concentration, but eventually two figures came into focus. A moment later his eyes closed again. He tried to breathe. That was all he could do . . . just lie there and breathe.

06

Aiden picked up the phone for the twelfth time in a week and crossed his fingers. Behind-the-desk Jessica always sounded happy to hear from him, but the news was not always good. The dog he'd rescued from the Collinses' yard was up and down by the day, and sometimes the hour.

"Hi, Jessica, it's me again." Aiden knew she recognized his voice, even if his number was "unknown." He hoped he wasn't bothering her too much—it wasn't as if the dog he'd brought in was the only creature they had to care for. MA Rescue was a busy place!

"Aiden, hi!" she said cheerfully. "I've been

waiting for your call all morning. I finally have some good news!"

Aiden uncrossed his fingers and let out his breath, which he hadn't realized he'd been holding. "Really?" he asked. "Let's hear it."

"Your little pup is off the IV, and he kept down some water and kibble on his own last night. Not much, mind you, but it's still a huge development. Oh, and he had a bowel movement!"

Aiden let out a laugh on his end of the phone. Poop! Surprisingly that was something to celebrate!

"He needs to stay here with us for a while longer, but Dr. Wells and Liam both agree he's definitely out of the woods. I imagine he'll be ready for adoption in a couple of weeks." She paused, and Aiden guessed that she was smiling on the other end of the line. "That little dog of yours is one tough cookie."

Aiden smiled into the phone, too. The word "yours" stuck in his mind, and he wished it was accurate. He'd like nothing more than to take the little guy into his home—the border collie was clearly already in his heart. But he knew it was out of the question, because his wife, Ruby, was allergic. Like, seriously allergic. The closest she could safely get to a dog was a YouTube video. No, this pup would not be his. He felt his stomach drop with disappointment but reminded himself that a week ago the pup was on death's door. Now he was a giant step closer to becoming *somebody's* cherished pet. It was fantastic news!

In the kennel area with a slew of other dogs, the little black-and-white pup let out a happy bark. He felt soooooo good! He was closed in a kennel four or five times the size of his tethered space in the old yard. He had a collar on, but it was made of soft material and felt loose around his neck, which wasn't as raw now that it had scabbed over and was starting to heal. And there was nothing else tied to him . . . no choker! The man who'd been caring for him since he woke up in this place brought him food many times a day and kept his water bowl full at all times. He hadn't forgotten once!

Speaking of water, the pup was a teensy bit

thirsty. He lifted himself off his comfy bed and bowed low and long in front, stretching his rear high in the air, then ambled over to the metal bowl. It was much bigger than the one he'd had in the yard, and he lapped up a good drink. Satisfied, he trotted over to the door of his kennel to watch the man who cared for him and another lady walk back and forth, bringing dogs in and out, weighing them, getting things out of cupboards, and writing stuff down. These people were busy!

The pup lay down on his belly and rested his head on his paws, which were a true white after a warm, soapy bath. He wondered how long he'd been here. It was hard to tell because the first few days were a big, fuzzy blur . . . He didn't really remember them at all. What he did remember was his life in the awful yard, the teasing, the dust, and the hot, hot sun. He remembered that the house went quiet and the boy stopped coming. After that things grew hazy. There was hunger and heat. Then a vague memory of someone finally coming to find him. And after that, he was here. Here!

Here was wonderful. Here was *amazing*. The only thing he didn't like here was when someone came to take him outside. Outside itself wasn't the problem—outside was nice. There was grass and dirt and plants and trees. But the only way to get outside was to let someone clip one of those things that could choke him at any moment—a choker—on his collar. And even though the little pup's neck didn't hurt as much, that binding leash made the memory of his old life come flooding back. It twisted his stomach and made the fur along his spine stand straight into the air. It made him feel all tied up. Tied up and teased or left alone and starved . . . almost to death. It was too much. He hated that leash. He'd rather stay in his kennel and pee and poop in the corner. It might be too close to his bed, but it was better than being attached to a choker. No, the pup would not go outside.

Liam finished making notes about a puffy orange Pomeranian with worms and put the clipboard on a hook on the wall. He picked up the border collie's leash and, half hiding it behind his

44

back, carried it over to his kennel. He'd noticed the rescued dog's fear and was going to try something new today . . . once they were outside. But first he had to get him there.

"Ready for your walk, buddy?" Liam asked quietly as he opened the kennel door. The little pup raced back to his bed in the corner and curled up into a tight ball.

Liam sighed inwardly but talked calmly and cheerfully to the dog. "Come on, now . . . it's all right." He walked slowly to the back of the kennel, crouched, and set the leash down behind him. He reached out a hand to stroke the fur on the dog's back—it was getting shinier every day. When the pup had relaxed a bit, Liam quickly grabbed the leash and clipped it onto the collar. "Come on, boy," Liam said, putting excitement in his voice. "Come on!"

Slowly the border collie got to his feet . . . sort of. He crouch-walked his way to the door, tail between his back legs and ears drooping. Liam basically had to drag him to the door. "I'm not torturing you," the tech said. Though it sure looked like he was.

Outside, the dog was too distracted to go to the bathroom, or even sniff anything. All he could do was stand there and think about the leash tied to his neck. What if it suddenly yanked him? What if Liam tied him up and left him? All the dog wanted was to get back to his kennel . . . to his water bowl and his bed.

Liam watched with a furrowed brow as the leashed pup quivered. The dog flinched badly whenever the leash moved or jostled his collar. Based on the little Liam knew about the dog's history, he made a guess.

"Can you play without this?" the tech asked, unclipping the leash.

The pup watched the leash disappear behind Liam's back and felt his lungs fill. He felt his tail and ears rise. All of a sudden he could smell the grass! He could hear the wind in the trees! His tail wagged and he sniffed the air.

Looking down at him, Liam smiled, but his happy expression soon shifted into one of anger.

He knew from instinct and experience that the happy dog in front of him was the real border collie . . . the cowering, flinching, and fear didn't come naturally to the breed, or any dog. It had been conditioned into him. He hated the way some people treated animals, and the way they tossed them aside when they became inconvenient!

Liam reached down to give the dog an ear stroke. "That's better, isn't it, boy?" he said. He pulled a tennis ball out of his pocket, wishing there was a way to make the poor pup's abused past disappear . . .

Spotting the toy, the pup was instantly on alert. His bicolored eyes locked onto the felted round thing in Liam's hand. He craned his neck and leaned forward. He lifted one paw, trembling. He wanted it baaad! He wanted that ball, ball, *Ball*!

Liam saw an intensity in the pup's eyes that hadn't been there before. The leash, along with the trauma it created, all but vanished. Liam tossed the tennis ball, and the pup sprinted after it and brought it back, dropping it at his feet without prompting. Liam threw the ball again and again and again. The pup seemed to speed toward the ball with jet-engine propulsion. It would have been hard to convince a passing stranger that this speedy dog had been on death's door a week ago! Liam smiled as he threw the ball over and over.

"You're like a jet!" Liam crowed happily. "Actually, I think you *are* Jet."

The happy dog opened his mouth, and the ball fell at Liam's feet for the umpteenth time. He let out an ecstatic bark. Liam laughed. "Okay! Glad we agree! Jet it is, then!"

Not paying attention, Liam threw the ball into a hedge, where it got caught between some gnarled branches on the far side. Jet was not deterred. He hurled his body headfirst into the bush, wriggling his hindquarters wildly, and emerged several seconds later with the ball clenched between his teeth and several leaves tangled in his fur. Liam watched him, amazed. Jet had some serious prey drive! He checked his watch, surprised to discover that they had been out here for more than half an hour.

"I've got to get back to work, Jet," he said a little

sadly. He pulled the leash from his pocket and Jet dropped instantly to the grass, looking like he wanted to sink into the earth altogether. All signs of the playful pup were gone in a flash.

"Hey, now, Jet," Liam said casually. He stepped toward the dog, ready to clip on the leash, but as he approached, the back door opened and Sofia, one of his coworkers, came out with another dog. Liam glanced her way and stepped toward Jet at the same time, not seeing that Jet's hackles were on high. Jet's eyes were fixed on the leash, and he was letting out a low growl.

"Better watch it, dog," Sofia said in passing. "That kind of behavior is a one-way ticket to—"

Liam's head shot up and Sofia, getting the message, didn't finish her sentence. But Liam knew she was right. Growling at people wasn't something that got a dog adopted. In fact, it was a big red flag . . . even when the behavior was caused by fear and not outright aggression. Fear, Liam knew, could cause major behavior issues. And trainers—even good ones—didn't always have the skill or patience to train it out of them. And in a shelter with limited space? Growling and fearful behaviors were basically a death sentence.

Liam's brows crowded together tightly. He'd gotten attached to the skinny doggo and wanted him to land on his feet—wanted him to have a shot at a better life. As Liam tugged him back to the door, he was flooded with regret. Just that morning he'd told Jessica that Jet would be ready for adoption soon, and she'd undoubtedly relayed the news to Aiden. Now it seemed as if he'd spoken too soon.

Now it seemed as if adoption might not be in Jet's future at all.

07

"Thanks for checking out the border collie!" Roxanne Valentine said, her voice echoing over the hands-free phone link in Georgia Sterling's car. Georgia, the daughter-in-law of founder Frances Sterling and the manager of daily operations at Sterling Center, was on a mission. In her regular job she managed the money, the publicity, and the people at the Sterling ranch, a place where lucky, "unadoptable" dogs were given the opportunity to channel their intelligence, speed, and energy into something valuable. After being recruited, dogs at Sterling went through months of intensive training to become search and rescue dogs.

Most of the staff on the ranch were members of Frances and Georgia's family—Georgia's husband, Martin, was in charge of maintenance and facilities, and their children actively helped care for the dogs or managed the front desk in the welcome center when they weren't in school. Her other staff members—educator of potential trainers Pedro Sundal, assistant dog trainer Eloise Green, and lead dog trainer extraordinaire Roxanne Valentine—rounded out the team with their skill and knowledge.

Under normal circumstances, Roxanne was the person who evaluated a prospective dog for recruitment. Right now, though, a couple of the canines she was working with were at key points in their training, and a full day away from the ranch could really impede their progress. So when the call came in from a young vet tech at Midland Animal Rescue, Georgia offered to make the trip and evaluate the dog herself. The tech, a man named Liam, had been insistent and convincing: "You have to see this dog. His prey drive is off the charts." Roxanne and

Georgia had both heard good things about MA Rescue, and border collies, as a breed, were well known in the working dog world. Sterling ranch had had successes with similar dogs in the past. Plus they were on the lookout for new canine recruits. So after the two women talked it over, they decided Georgia should make the trip.

Georgia wasn't alone on this mission, either. She turned to look at her middle daughter, Morgan, who was gazing out the window as they sped along the California highway.

"We're happy to do it," Georgia told Roxanne over the speakerphone.

"Suuuuper happy!" Morgan agreed.

Truth be told, Morgan was the real expert. Or at the least an expert in training. Aside from eight-year-old Juniper, who was 100 percent team cat, Georgia's children were all dedicated to dogs. But it was eleven-year-old Morgan who had the right combination of intuition, drive, and skill to make her an actual handler. Georgia suspected that Morgan would make dogs and dog training her lifelong passion. She took after her grandmother Frances, with a little bit of Roxanne—and possibly actual dog—mixed in.

"Can't wait to hear how it goes. Talk to you later!" Roxanne hung up, and Morgan checked the map on her phone.

"Turn left in half a mile, on Ash," she instructed. They'd been driving for several hours and were finally nearing their destination. Evaluating dogs often involved hundreds of miles and an entire day, and at last they were here. As they pulled into the parking lot Morgan tried to contain her excitement. She had never been asked to participate in assessing a dog and knew it was a huge responsibility. She was honored, excited, and more than a teensy bit nervous!

They were barely inside the door before a vet tech in paw-print scrubs was in front of them, vigorously shaking their hands. "Thank you, both, so much for coming! I just know the Sterling Center is the right place for Jet."

"I take it you're the one who called?" Georgia

asked, collecting her mass of loose black curls and pulling it over one shoulder. She smiled, revealing dimples and crinkling the skin at the corners of her warm dark eyes.

"Oh!" Liam suddenly looked embarrassed. "I'm sorry! I have no manners! I'm Liam. And yes, I'm the one who called."

From behind the desk, Jessica let out a small laugh. "He's a little in love with the dog in question," she said. "He really can't help himself."

Liam blushed while the receptionist introduced herself. "I'm Jessica," she told them. After their hellos, Liam led Georgia and Morgan to the kennels.

"I've been calling him Jet because he's so fast—especially when chasing a ball . . ."

Jet lifted his head at the sound of Liam's voice. His ears stood at attention. He hoped Ball was in his pocket. He trotted to the front of his kennel and took a big sniff. He couldn't tell if Liam had Ball or just smelled like Ball, but he could tell there were other people with him . . . new people.

"Oh!" Morgan dropped to her knee when she

spotted the dog, instantly in love. The black-and-white border collie mix with one blue and one brown eye wagged at her (and Liam, no doubt) from the other side of the chain-link gate. Though his ribs were still visible, even under his patchy mid-length fur, he was obviously curious and full of energy. His eyes were as twinkly as sparklers!

Georgia crouched next to her daughter. "What's not to love about this guy?" she asked. "You're so handsome!" she cooed to the pup.

The young dog stretched his neck and licked Morgan's fingers, which were wrapped around the kennel links. "Who wouldn't want to take you home?" Georgia said in a low, playful voice.

Liam smiled, watching them. These were serious dog people, and they seemed to like Jet. But he knew what Georgia was saying. Though Jet was not a super-young puppy, which most people came looking for, the black-and-white border collie with the floppy ears and mismatched eyes appeared to be highly adoptable . . . Why the urgent call? As he considered the question, his smile faded. He may as well show them what the issue was; there was no sense putting it off.

The moment the leash appeared in Jet's line of sight, the Sterlings understood. The change in the dog was immediate and extreme. His fear was so strong that even if they hadn't been able to see it, all three humans could feel it in the air. Jet skittered back to his bed and curled up into a ball, cowering.

Georgia's smile faded. She'd really hoped this would work out.

Morgan's eyes glistened—she felt for the poor pup. "What happened to you?" she asked the shivering dog.

"They found him tied up in a backyard . . . nearly starved to death," Liam explained. "He was probably tethered most of his life." He stepped inside the kennel and approached Jet with the leash hidden in his back pocket. The pup let the tech come close, accepted a pet, and allowed him to clip on the leash. Still, as he did so, Morgan thought she heard a low growl rumbling in the back of his throat. She did a double take—he looked so timid—and glanced at her mom to see if she'd heard the same thing. Growling was a bad sign, but her mom either didn't notice or didn't say anything, and Jet was quiet now that the leash was on.

Liam spoke sweetly to Jet and moved slowly. He led Jet closer to the visitors, who smelled like dogs. With his tail down, Jet walked outside with the three humans.

As soon as they were all outside Liam let him off the leash. Since there wasn't a ball in sight, Jet wandered over to his regular relief spots and took care of business—not a problem when he wasn't tied. Then he trotted back to the people to see what would happen next . . . and saw exactly what he was hoping for. Ball, Ball, *Ball*!

"Arf!" Jet let out a bark before sitting down and waiting as patiently as he could. His bottom wiggled on the grass. Ball!

"This is where his prey drive really kicks in," Liam said. He handed the ball to Morgan, who threw it several times. Jet went after it like a dynamo.

"Wow," Georgia said, surprised at the quick

change in attitude. "He's definitely enthusiastic! Does he show aggression toward other dogs?"

Liam shook his head. "He doesn't. And not around food, either."

Georgia's eyebrows went up while her mouth curled down in consideration. "That's unusual in a dog who's been starved."

Morgan held the ball in her hand for several seconds longer than usual, looking for the perfect, difficult-to-get place to throw it. She needed to see what Jet would do if the ball were hard to reach—how driven he really was. She needed her mom to see his potential. She looked around, settling on the hedge in the far corner. She threw the ball, hitting the tangle of branches about three feet off the ground head-on and trapping the ball in the center. Bull's-eye!

Jet sprinted toward the hedge, barely slowing down as he approached. His eyes were on one thing and one thing only: Ball! When his front paws were within a couple of feet, he paused the slightest bit, leaped into the air, and shoved his snout into the tangle of branches. His teeth clamped around Ball a split second before his back legs touched the ground. He landed and yanked his head out at the same time, still holding Ball and shaking it triumphantly from side to side.

Georgia let out a whistle. "Impressive," she said.

After trotting back to Morgan with his head high, Jet dropped Ball at her feet and gave a bark, ready to go again.

"Can you distract him, Liam?" Morgan asked. "I want to see if I can hide the ball out of sight."

"No problem." Liam called over another tech, who was walking an Australian shepherd mix named Kota, and encouraged Jet to greet them. Jet didn't even glance at the other dog. In fact he didn't take his eyes off Morgan . . . or the ball. It was like Kota wasn't even there.

Morgan put the ball behind her back and tried to switch hands. No matter what she did, she couldn't get Jet to look away from the ball for even a single moment. That kind of focus, Morgan knew, was ideal for a working dog.

"This is definitely a dog who wants a job!" Georgia laughed.

"So, we're taking him?" Morgan's heart soared. Jet had so much potential; he just needed a chance. She threw the ball and looked quickly back at her mom.

Georgia looked unsure. "Drive isn't everything, Schatz," she told her daughter, using her second language, German, as she sometimes did. "You saw how timid he was earlier, how he reacted to the leash."

Morgan gulped. She'd seen it. And she'd heard it. "That's because he hasn't had any training yet." She tried to make it seem like it wasn't a big deal. She hoped it wasn't a big deal. She hoped her mom would agree to take Jet to the ranch with them! "He deserves a chance."

Georgia looked at her kindhearted daughter's face. Of course she agreed, every dog needed a chance. But she also had to make wise decisions and not waste her staff's time, or the dog's. Though he was obviously high-energy, Jet still seemed adoptable to her.

"I *know* we can train him," Morgan added. If she *hoped* hard enough was it the same as knowing?

Jet raced back to them with his ball, dropped it at Morgan's feet, and looked eagerly at it, eyes alight. Morgan studied her mom's face with equal intensity. Even Liam was looking expectantly at Georgia. There was only one answer she could give. Georgia nodded slowly. "Okay. We'll take him."

Morgan exhaled and let out a whoop. She'd just helped recruit her first dog!

08

The car ride was the longest Jet had ever taken. He still didn't like the grumbling engine noise or the gasoline smells, but at least on this ride he didn't lose his lunch. He stood in the crate with his snout pointed toward the woman and girl in the front seats, inhaling their scents for a long time. He liked the way they smelled. The girl was like a smaller version of the woman, with twisted hair that looked like tiny ropes instead of loopy curls. They both smelled of lavender and coffee and something spicy he'd never laid his nose on. They also smelled like dogs. Well, not exactly like dogs, because they were humans. But it was clear that they spent time around dogs—a lot of time and a lot of dogs! It was deeply reassuring. After sniffing his fill, Jet curled into a circle and slept. He didn't wake up until the car slowed to a stop in a parking lot.

The girl opened one of the car doors and unlatched the crate. She held one hand behind her back and patted her leg with the other. "Come on, boy," she coaxed.

Jet didn't need any convincing to get out of the car. He jumped down and shook off the sleep and the long ride.

"Can you take him to the pavilion, honey?" the coffee-scented woman asked. She gathered up bags and paperwork and headed toward the door of the nearest building.

"On it!" the girl replied. She bent down to give Jet a pat. "Just wait until you see your new place. You're going to love it." Jet dipped his chin and accepted the petting. He liked the way the girl talked to him—in a kind voice, and no yelling. And he liked her gentle hands.

The woman looked back over her shoulder. "Put

a leash on him so he doesn't run off!" she called. "He wouldn't know where to come back to!"

"Okay," the girl replied, reaching for her pocket. But the moment the woman turned away, the girl brought her hands out in front of her again. They were empty. "You don't need a leash, do you?" she asked in a low voice. She didn't want to see the sweet border collie tremble in fear again—especially right now when he was being introduced to his new home.

"I know you're going to like it here. It's a happy place for pups, and there's nothing to be afraid of. Just wait until you meet Roxanne!" Morgan talked in her soothing, playful voice. It made Jet curious to see more. Already he loved how this place smelled— so much greener and damper than the yard he'd lived in. It was cooler here, too.

Jet followed the girl, cautiously, curiously, picking up a little more confidence with each step. The place was a sniffer's paradise! It was loaded with smells he didn't recognize, and also some he did: dogs, trees, grass, food, children, cats, dirt, wood, squirrels . . . He breathed in and out, trying to fill his short snout with as much information as he could take in. When he paused on the path to linger over a smell, the girl would pat her leg to encourage him along, so Jet stayed close, and when she opened the door to a big building he got a whole new noseful!

"Welcome to the canine pavilion!" Morgan swept her arm around a huge, garage-like room. Sunlight streamed in from overhead windows, lighting up the kennels that lined one side of the building. It looked and smelled a lot like the place where Jet had just been, only these kennels were bigger and had dog-sized doors that opened to small yards outside.

"Hey, Morgan!" a boy wearing rubber boots called out. He looked a lot like the girl but was taller with shorter hair and lighter eyes. He was holding a hose, and the pup was tempted to run up and get a drink. He was thirsty!

"That the new recruit?" He squatted down, set aside the hose, and patted his leg like Morgan had. Jet walked up to him slowly.

"Forrest, meet Jet. Jet, this is Forrest," Morgan introduced the dog to her thirteen-year-old brother. Jet let the boy ruffle his fur but felt a bit uneasy. Did this boy tease like his first boy? The thought made him want to whine, so he wandered away and sniffed the perimeter of the place. There were a lot of dogs in the big kennels, many of whom greeted him with happy wags and nose touches through the fencing.

"You're back!" Jet whirled when he heard a new voice. A tall woman with pale, speckled skin walked in, followed by another child, smaller than Forrest and Morgan. The woman gazed at Jet intently, narrowing her eyes. Jet could tell she was sizing him up. But not in a challenging way. Jet sniffed her tennis shoes and moved on quickly, because the young girl behind her was holding something *really* interesting . . . a cat!

Jet had never been this close to a cat before. In the yard he'd smelled them on the other side of the fence. He'd even see them slinking through the yard at a safe distance. Jet thought cats smelled amazing and was excited to finally get a closer sniff! He stepped up to the striped beast draped over the child's arm and inhaled. The big orange cat sniffed him back, unimpressed.

"So, should I start with heeling first or sitting first?" the young girl asked. "Is there a proper order to learn obedience? I mean, I've been teaching them some things I learned on YouTube, but I think my kitties are ready for more serious training." The cat girl talked fast and didn't pause for a second when Jet approached. She seemed as unimpressed by the new dog as her cat was! She barely acknowledged Jet, glancing down briefly before flipping one of her braids over her shoulder and peppering the speckled woman with more questions. The edges of the woman's mouth curled up and her eyes twinkled playfully. She touched her hair, which was pulled together like a tail on the back of her head.

Roxanne held back a giggle. Her dog-training skills were top-notch, no question. But did dog-training techniques translate to *cat* training? She doubted it but actually had no idea. She was only sure of one thing: Juniper, the youngest Sterling, was going to find out. Juniper wanted to train her two cats, Twig and Bud, the way the Sterlings trained rescue dogs, and she would not be deterred. The eight-year-old was unstoppable.

"I think you should start with a basic sit command," Roxanne suggested. "Leash training a cat might be . . . challenging."

Morgan slowly shook her head. She tried to imagine Twig, or *any* cat, listening to commands. It seemed unlikely, but if there was a human alive who could make a cat do her bidding, it was Juniper.

Ignoring the conversation, Forrest, who frequently tuned out his sisters, knelt down to get a read on the new dog. He was used to canine recruits warming up to him instantly. Morgan was admittedly *every* dog's best friend, but Forrest was almost always a close second. This dog, though, was definitely cool on him.

"Here, Jet," he called softly, and held his hand out so the border collie could sniff him. He made sure to keep his hands visible and not reach up above the dog's line of sight when he petted him. Jet submitted to the touch, but Forrest could still sense his wariness. He wondered what his life had been like before now. That was the thing with rescue dogs—you never knew what they'd been through. "You've got pretty eyes," Forrest crooned, dipping his head to look at them. Jet dipped his head, too, and looked away.

"Two-tone!" Roxanne exclaimed, catching a glimpse. "If you were my dog, I'd name you Bowie!"

"Oh, Jet fits him!" Morgan looked around for a ball. "Let me show you!"

"Good idea," Roxanne said. "Let's take him to the training grounds so I can see what he's got. Get a lead on him and let's go!"

Jet saw Morgan and Forrest perk up, and his own ears lifted. The little one with the cat just sniffed. Jet thought about giving the cat another once-over with his nose but was suddenly distracted by something in Morgan's hand—Ball!

Morgan pocketed a tennis ball and started to reach for the leash in her back pocket. Then she stopped. She wanted Roxanne to see where Jet excelled before she saw the work that would have to be done. She shoved the coiled leash in deeper and headed for the door. "I forgot his leash, but he's great at heeling," she called over her shoulder, trying to sound casual.

"We have more leads here . . ." Roxanne pointed toward the wall where at least a dozen leashes were hanging. Leashing dogs was standard procedure on the ranch . . . especially with new dogs. Fortunately Morgan was already halfway gone with Jet on her heels.

"I'll take her one!" Juniper grabbed a leash off the wall and raced after her sister, calling her name. "Mooorgaaan!" Morgan stopped. Jet stopped with her, waiting as patiently as he could for the first toss of Ball. Turning, Morgan saw Juniper sprinting toward her, dark braids flying, with a cat over one arm and a leash in the opposite hand. Feeling a flash of panic, she stepped between her little sister and the dog . . . too late.

Jet saw the leash and instantly flattened himself

to the ground. Cringing, Morgan glanced toward the pavilion. Roxanne was just outside the door. Morgan wanted to block both Jet's and Roxanne's views, but Juniper sidestepped Morgan and reached for the dog's collar while holding the leash.

Juniper didn't think there was anything unusual about the dog lying down to get his leash on, but Morgan saw the panic in Jet's eyes. Then, even worse, she saw his lip quiver and start to curl. A low growl was forming in his throat when Morgan snatched the lead from her sister before she could clip it and hid it under her shirt. "Let's go, Jet!" she called, holding out the ball and starting to run.

Jet was instantly relieved. The choker leash was nowhere to be seen, and Morgan had Ball! He jumped up to follow her, and the two raced to the training grounds with Forrest, Roxanne, Juniper, and Twig following shortly behind.

09

Pedro Sundal closed the door to the one-bedroom trailer he called home and made his way along the path toward the center of Sterling ranch. He'd kicked around at different jobs before coming here a few years ago and had never been happier. Working alongside the Sterling family and Roxanne Valentine, training humans and dogs to become search and rescue teams was the best job he'd had, hands down. It was a dream come true. Though the joke on the ranch was that he had the harder job— training the humans as opposed to the dogs—he'd always been a people person and had a knack for pairing people with the right canine companions.

As he strolled past the mock bus wreck he heard excited voices—lots of them—and decided to take a quick detour. Though excited voices were certainly nothing new on the ranch, something told him that *this* was a moment he didn't want to miss. As he got closer he heard happy barks along with the shouts. A smile bloomed on his sun-kissed face before he'd even caught a glimpse of the fun.

On the wide training grounds, Pedro saw Roxanne and three of the four Sterling kids. Twig was also in attendance. Then he saw what was making them all shout and cheer; a young black-and-white border collie was tearing after a ball with surprising speed and skill. The dog was skinny and looked like he'd seen hard days, but he obviously wasn't letting that slow him down. He moved at lightning speed and interacted with the ball as if it was a magnet and he was metal. The dog could predict where the ball was going before it got there, running past the hurled object and turning just in time to snag it in his teeth.

"Wow!" Pedro clapped, impressed after only

three tosses. The dog had the focus and drive of a professional athlete. "Nice dog," he commented, joining Roxanne. Neither of them took their eyes off the canine recruit for more than a moment. Roxanne was nodding appreciatively. She'd been working with dogs for a long time and knew extraordinary skill and speed when she saw them. This new pup had both in spades. She turned and smiled at Pedro. The two operated like right and left hands on the ranch—she with the dogs and he with the humans—and together they made great search and rescue teams. They were so in sync they often communicated in silence, using only their eyes and body language.

"He's got the drive!" Roxanne agreed. "And agility won't be an issue . . ." Her phone beeped in her pocket and she glanced at it, letting the "but" that Pedro sensed might be coming fall away.

"It's late!" she said, noticing the time. She'd lost track watching the exuberance of the new dog . . . and thinking. "Let's go!" she called to the whole gang, waving them over. It was time to clean up for dinner, and she had to make a few notes in the pavilion before that.

Jet hated to see the game end, but he'd had so much fun he didn't mind too much. He didn't know what he liked best . . . the running, the jumping, the twisting in midair, the connecting with Ball, or the victorious return to the children with it clasped safely in his jaw. Actually, he did know. His favorite part was the freedom to run Ball down without being choked back! He bounded over to Roxanne along with the kids, tail up, his pink tongue sticking out from underneath Ball. He felt waggy all over!

Roxanne watched the pup approach and lifted the leash off her arm to attach it to his collar.

The moment Jet saw it, everything changed. He stopped dead in his tracks. His waggy feeling was gone. She stepped closer to him with her hand extended. Her voice was kind, but Jet could barely hear it. He was as focused on the leash as he had been on Ball, which fell from his mouth as he dropped to the ground, flattening himself on the spring grass. He did not want the choker. He did not want to be trapped. He did not want to be tied up and left to die. Ever. Again.

Roxanne's brow furrowed, and her lips disappeared between her teeth. "Mmm." She didn't have the words for the thoughts racing so quickly through her head. She recognized the leash fear for what it was. "It's okay, Jet," she finally said. She put the leash in her pocket and watched the young dog's demeanor change. The happy pup he'd been a moment before was back. Pedro looked at her, and Roxanne saw the silent questions in his thoughtful brown eyes. She had them, too. "At least I hope it's okay," she added softly.

10

The next morning Morgan woke up early. It was Sunday, and she wanted to finish the homework she'd put off to evaluate Jet. After that she'd be spending as much time as possible with the dog she helped choose! She stretched her arms over her head and rolled onto her side. Her older sister, Shelby, was still asleep, and snoring, in the twin bed on the other side of the room. She was completely hidden by her covers except for one foot, which dangled over the edge of the mattress.

Ever since she'd turned fourteen—and even more so now that she was fifteen—Shelby had become a champion sleeper. Like Olympic caliber. Gone were the days when the two of them would sneak downstairs early to watch Netflix together (in a family of six it wasn't always easy to get everyone to agree on what was bingeworthy). The two of them used to be on the same page about most things, but not so much anymore. Shelby valued sleeping in on weekends above all else, and Morgan knew better than to try to wake her.

Morgan stood and tiptoed out of the room, opening the door and stepping into the hall. She stopped when she heard voices downstairs in the kitchen. Roxanne and Pedro were here and having a conversation with her mom. The two of them were over at the Sterlings' house a lot, and talked to her mom a lot, too. The ranch employees were practically family and came for dinner regularly. But Sunday mornings were not one of their regular times. People at the ranch worked hard but usually took Sundays off. Judging by the serious tones and lack of laughter, this was business. Emergency business.

Morgan swallowed hard and backed into her bedroom, leaving the door open a crack. She sat down on the end of Shelby's bed that was closer to the heating vent that connected to the kitchen, to try to hear what the adults were saying. Shelby stopped snoring and started kicking.

"Sorry!" Morgan sat down on the floor and stretched to get an ear close to the vent. She wanted to hear what they were talking about. She was also afraid she already knew.

"He's talented. And driven." Roxanne's muffled voice came through the duct. "But he's also *very* fearful," she added. "And fear is an extremely hard thing to train out of a dog. Remember Race?"

Morgan could practically see Pedro's and her mom's heads bobbing as well as the pained expressions on their faces. They all remembered Race.

Morgan twisted the hem of her pajama shorts, thinking about the sweet brown dog. There were not a lot of "failures" on the ranch, but Race had been one. Roxanne and her assistants worked with the chocolate Lab for days and weeks and months in an effort to train away his trust issues. But in the end Race had been unable to overcome his fear.

He was skittish and unpredictable. The SAR dog and handler relationship was, by nature, intense. Both partners had to be willing to trust the other with everything—with their *lives*. For Race, fear trumped trust every time.

Happily, Race was adopted into a family in the next county over, and everyone on the ranch was glad to know he was living a good life. But none of them ever really got over the loss of potential. Race had the nose and drive of a champion rescuer. Years later it wasn't so much that Race had failed them, but the feeling that everyone at the ranch had failed *him*. And they had wasted precious time and resources doing it.

"I'm concerned that even *if* Jet's fear is something we can overcome—and that's a big if—it will take more time and energy than the trainers and I can spare. It might be a waste of everyone's time."

Morgan stopped twisting her jammies. She stopped breathing, too.

There was a long pause before Roxanne added something that made Morgan's stomach clench. "It's my fault. You're the best manager I've ever known, Georgia, but dog behavior isn't your specialty. And though Morgan is knowledgeable beyond her years, she's still just a kid. I should have gone to evaluate Jet myself."

The tightness in Morgan's gut turned to pain. "Just a kid." She hated those words. She was grateful that most of the time her parents and her ranch family treated her like more than "just a kid." But had she acted like one? It was true that when she met Jet she wanted him to be a perfect rescue candidate. She wanted to identify a great recruit. Had she overlooked his shortcomings? Had she made a foolish decision? Was she just an immature . . . *kid*? And worse, was Jet about to be sent away before he got started?

Morgan heard Pedro's low lilting response. She didn't bother to try to make out the words or tiptoe out of the room. She jumped to her feet and raced down the stairs, bursting into the kitchen. "We can't send him back!" she blurted.

Morgan's father, Martin, was standing at the sink.

He wasn't a part of the emergency meeting, but he'd been listening and hadn't realized Morgan was listening, too.

"Aren't you interrupting?" Martin asked, his light eyebrows rising toward his receding hairline.

Morgan balled her hands into fists. She was, but . . . "It's just that I helped make the decision to bring Jet here, and I think he deserves a chance."

Roxanne, Pedro, and even her mom were all looking at Morgan with such sad eyes she was afraid she might start to cry, which wouldn't help her make her point. Her dad was no better. He had the biggest weepy cartoon eyes of all!

Martin squeezed his daughter's shoulder, wishing he could squeeze in some understanding and make this easier for her. He knew she would give her all to every dog, every mouse, and every *flea* to make sure they had the chance to live their best lives. That was his girl.

"I'm sorry I interrupted, but if you'll just listen . . ." Morgan tried again.

Georgia raised her eyebrows and indicated a seat

at the table. Morgan slid into the chair, looking sheepish. "It's just that, I have a few ideas. And I'm willing to do the work."

"We're listening, honey," Georgia said encouragingly. "None of us want Jet to have to leave, but if he's not a good prospect, we'll be wasting a lot of time, both his and ours. And money."

"So, I read this thing about leash fear and how to break it. They said at the shelter that he'd been tied up and abandoned. And probably tortured, too. When he sees a leash that's what he thinks of. But if we can change his association with leashes and ropes and tethers and stuff it should make him less afraid." She explained the recent videos she'd watched and how she thought she could approach the problem. "Once he knows that he's safe now, with us, and later with his handler, it will change everything. Also, I want to do it. I want to put in the time. I was the one who was so sure we should take a chance on Jet."

Roxanne nodded almost imperceptibly along with everything Morgan laid out. It took almost five minutes to tell them all her ideas—and Roxanne could tell that Morgan had done significant research. Most of the techniques she suggested were familiar to the veteran trainer, but some had impressive new twists. And Roxanne had to admit, Morgan volunteering her own time would be a big help.

Georgia's brow got smoother the longer Morgan talked.

Pedro smiled into his lap. Morgan could be convincing, and he, for one, was convinced.

"So?" Morgan tapped her foot impatiently under the table, waiting for an answer. She was so anxious she felt like she could—

"Aaaaaaaaah!" a shriek pierced the silence and made everyone around the table jump . . . even Morgan. She'd *wanted* to scream, but definitely hadn't. The cry had come from the floor above them! Everyone in the kitchen raced to the stairs and nearly ran headlong into Forrest, who was on his way down. Judging by the look of shock and horror on his face, he was the screamer.

"Was in aller Welt?" Georgia asked, the language

of her youth emerging. That tended to happen when she was rattled. Having emigrated from Eritrea to Germany as a young child, German was practically her first language. "I mean, why in the world are you screaming, Liebchen?" She grabbed Forrest and held him close to try to calm him down. Forrest allowed her to hug him for about two seconds. Then he shook her off and leaned against the wall, pointing toward Shelby and Juniper, who were standing on the top step with sleep in their eyes.

"I—I—I . . . up there, I just saw Bud using the *toilet* . . . our toilet!" he stuttered.

"You what?" Martin asked. "Are you sure you weren't dreaming?"

Juniper (who for once wasn't holding one or both of the cats) grinned widely and planted her hands on her hips. "That was no dream," she said smugly. "My kitty toilet training is finally working!"

11

On Monday Morgan raced through her homework, grateful that she didn't have as much as usual. As she whipped through her last assignment, her mind kept flitting to Jet. She had to work hard to force herself to think about science.

"There!" she finally said, slapping her pencil down on the kitchen table triumphantly. She scooped up the pages and hurried over to the welcome center in search of her mom. Part of the deal she'd struck on Sunday was that before she could do any extra work with Jet, she had to take care of her responsibilities. And school was at the top of that list.

"I'm done," Morgan panted, out of breath, as she

burst into the office where Georgia could be found most days. She held the pages out. Her mom took off her computer glasses and reached for them slowly. She peered at the hastily written answers, taking her time, and after a minute handed them back with a weak smile. Morgan was living up to her part of the bargain, but Georgia wasn't thrilled that her daughter was so dead set on training a *fearful* dog. Fear in dogs could be dangerous! Scared dogs, even sweet ones, reacted with a fight-or-flight response—in their frightened minds they were in a fight for their lives and would bite without thinking. Still, she couldn't deny her daughter. The girl was thoughtful and hardworking, and was a diligent dog-training student. When they'd discussed the plan, Morgan had a counterpoint for every one of Georgia's objections. If her career as a dog trainer didn't work out, Georgia thought, Morgan would make a pretty tough lawyer.

"Okay." Georgia's weak smile grew stronger and spread across her face. "If you're sure that's everything."

"It is," Morgan said, grinning back. "So I can—"

"You'll be *very* careful?" her mom interrupted to ask.

"I will!" Morgan crossed her heart like they did in Girl Scout camp whenever they made a promise. "Super careful."

Georgia nodded with her eyes closed. When she opened them she slowly shook her head as she watched her very determined daughter turn and hurry toward the canine pavilion.

Morgan made an important stop on her way. On the edge of the training grounds, she carefully coiled a leash on the ground. She set a treat in the center of the loops and made a silent wish that her plan would work. Building trust was slow work, Morgan knew, but she didn't have a lot of time. While she'd managed to convince the adults that she was up for the task of working with Jet on his leash fear, she knew her mom was worried. And Roxanne was skeptical. Plus, they'd given her a deadline: She had only five weeks to show a significant change in the dog's behavior around leashes. If Jet wasn't overcoming his fears by then, they wouldn't consider him for rescue training.

"Training a dog takes a lot of time and a lot of money," Roxanne had told Morgan—not that the girl needed reminding. She knew that her grandma Frances Sterling had started the facility with only volunteers and donations. Grandma had drilled into her head that every dollar and every hour spent on a dog was an investment. Everyone at Sterling was aware that they had to be careful with their resources, and spending time training a dog who was not going to make it through certification would be considered a waste. After all, the dogs they trained successfully would go on to save lives!

But Jet was not a waste! Morgan felt it in her bones. Yes, he'd had a rough start in life and hadn't been given a fair shake. But his drive was clear. He had real rescue dog potential, and Morgan refused to believe that any dog was too broken to find love and purpose.

"There you are!" Morgan walked into the pavilion confidently and greeted Jet with a playful voice.

She dropped her head a little and didn't look him in the eye, which could be considered aggressive. She didn't want to challenge him . . . at least not like that. She opened the kennel and held her hands down, inviting him out.

Jet wagged his hello. He was glad to see Morgan again and hoped they were going to play. With Ball!

After giving Jet a treat and a good petting to start a positive association with the training session, Morgan stood up. She walked past the wall of leashes and took a ball from the basket of toys they kept in the pavilion. Jet followed her with his eyes. He'd been paying attention before, but once she had a muddy tennis ball in her hands he was locked onto her every move. He stood at attention, his right front paw hovering just above the floor.

"No leash needed!" Morgan said quietly to herself.

Jet followed her out to the grounds, his eyes riveted on the dingy tennis ball. His whole body wiggled as he waited for her to throw it. He wanted to watch it leave her hand. He wanted to chase it. He wanted to catch it!

"We're just going to play today," Morgan said. She sent the ball sailing across the large open area, and Jet took off after it. Morgan wanted today's time together to be filled with games. She wanted Jet to associate training time with fun, which for most dogs it really was.

"Again?" she asked Jet when he dropped the slobbery ball at her feet. Jet was practically vibrating with anticipation. She offered him a treat. He'd been starved as a puppy, and she'd observed that he was treat-driven as well as prey-driven. For the moment, though, the ball was all he wanted. "Okay," Morgan said, laughing. She hurled the ball again, this time sending it toward the spot where she'd left the coiled leash.

She had hoped that the treat perched in the center of the wound-up lead would entice Jet to at least approach the feared item, but now she realized that food probably wouldn't do it. Still, she wanted to try again. The next time Jet returned the ball, Morgan tossed it so lightly that it rolled onto the coiled leash. Bull's-eye.

Jet bounded after Ball. Morgan held her breath. But the second Jet caught sight of the leash he skidded to a halt and began to back away. A choker! Even lying on the ground it brought back the awful memories. He wanted Ball, but not enough to go near the choker . . . Jet took another step backward, and then another.

"Jet!" Morgan called. She approached the terrified pup, talking in a soothing voice. Jet didn't hear her, though. He took one last look at the torture device lying on the ground and bolted away from her as fast as his four legs would carry him.

12

"Hey, Mom!" Martin Sterling greeted his mother. "You're just in time." The tall man hugged Frances with one arm while balancing a steaming bowl of Mexican rice in the other.

"It smells great in here!" Frances said as she stepped into the kitchen. The white-haired woman felt at home in her son's house and immediately busied herself with helping to get the food on the table. She came for dinner most nights and appreciated the controlled chaos of her four grandchildren as well as her daughter-in-law's fantastic cooking.

Shelby, her oldest grandchild, sauntered into the already crowded kitchen and kissed her grandma on the cheek. "I'll grab the napkins," she offered.

The seven Sterlings took their seats around the oval dining table, which was loaded down with burrito bowl fixings.

"Beans, please!" Juniper called out. She liked her bowl layered in a very specific order, starting with black beans. The dishes went around, followed by salsas and hot sauce (extra for Georgia and Morgan), and Frances soaked in the happy sounds of clinking silverware and side conversations.

"How's the training going?" Frances asked when everyone was served. She'd been wondering about Morgan's recent endeavor with Jet, the new border collie. But it was Juniper who spoke up first.

"It's going stupendously! My cats are geniuses," she said, throwing her shoulders back proudly while simultaneously forking up a big bite.

Frances didn't doubt it.

"It doesn't take a genius to use a toilet," Forrest said with his own mouth full. Burrito bowls were a family favorite. Georgia shot him a look, and Forrest chewed and swallowed before adding, "They can't even flush."

Juniper's shoulders slumped and she pouted, annoyed. She'd never understand why her family was so gaga about dogs but didn't appreciate the infinite superiority of cats.

"Maybe this isn't the best dinner conversation," Martin said in an effort to steer the table talk away from all things bathroom.

"Using the toilet isn't *all* the cats can do," Juniper insisted. "Twig can fetch now!"

"And how is that supposed to help him rescue people?" Shelby asked, unable to contain her eye roll. Juniper was cute with her cats, but did she honestly think cats could compete with dogs when it came to finding and saving human beings? Cats didn't have noses like dogs, and more importantly, they weren't that interested in helping people . . . or working.

"Also, they're really amazing at sleeping in the sun!" Forrest piled on, impersonating his littlest sister and cracking himself up. "I can't *wait* to see them on leashes!" He laughed. "Maybe you can use string!"

Martin gave his son a look, silently telling him to tone it down. Juniper hated to be teased.

Morgan watched Juniper's face screw up into a scowl. It wasn't easy being the youngest of four—as second youngest, she knew. "I've been fetching with Jet, too," she offered. "Retrieving is an important training step. It shows drive."

Juniper's face softened and she looked at Morgan gratefully. "Yeah," she said.

"And how's it going with Jet and the leash?" Georgia asked, turning toward Morgan.

Morgan scooped a big bite of rice and beans into her mouth. By throwing Juniper a bone she'd accidentally moved herself into the hot seat. Chewing would give her a moment to think. She hadn't told anyone about Jet bolting on Monday, or that it had taken her forty minutes to locate him. Even after she found him by the giant tower of rubble where dogs practiced agility, it had taken another fifteen minutes to coax him back to the pavilion. The whole thing had been completely disheartening. She knew she couldn't expect a miracle on the first day, but . . .

Morgan swallowed her bite and her worry in one gulp. "So far, so good," she reported. It wasn't completely untrue. She and Jet had done better today. She'd taken a different approach—one that didn't end in a wild-goose chase all over the ranch!—and left him in his kennel. She sat on one side of the chain-link gate with a leash while Jet stayed on the other. He kept his distance at first—sitting at the far end of the enclosure and regarding her warily. Morgan talked to him through the fencing. She showed him his ball and offered treats. Slowly he came close . . . close enough to take a treat from her outstretched fingers. And eventually he'd lain down with nothing but the metal mesh between him and Morgan and the leash. But the moment she touched the leash he'd sprung up and retreated back to the far end. Still, he'd come close. Closer, anyway.

"He's making headway," she said honestly.

The dinner chatter shifted to Shelby's English essay; their parents were wondering why she'd spent all afternoon on her phone when it was due tomorrow. Morgan only half listened, her brain churning while she crunched a tortilla chip and nodded to herself. Forrest's teasing comment about using string for leashing Twig and Bud had given her an idea.

🐾 🐾 🐾

Morgan was so anxious to try her new training idea that school on Friday seemed to go on forever. Luckily since she had the weekend ahead of her, she wasn't required to finish her homework before heading out to the pavilion and Jet!

"Hey, doggers!" she called to all the pups. They wagged their hellos, and Morgan made a beeline for Jet's kennel, walking past the hanging leashes without selecting one. She had all she needed: a ratty tennis ball and a secret surprise hidden in her fist.

Jet peered at Morgan suspiciously. Every time

they were together he saw a choker. Chokers held him in the place where he was taunted and starved. Chokers were not to be trusted. Ever. He looked Morgan over and inhaled her lavender scent mixed with the smell of the school bus, books, pencil shavings, and Ball!

"You want this?" she asked, holding up the shaggy tennis ball.

Jet froze. His eyes locked on Ball. Yes, he did!

He kept his eyes on the ball as they walked without a leash to the training grounds. Morgan was a little nervous that Jet might bolt again, but was willing to risk it. She threw the ball and watched Jet sail after it. He was so fast it looked like his paws didn't touch the ground! After a few throws she opened her fist and let Jet smell the surprise. It was a piece of balled-up yarn. It didn't look like a leash all wadded up like that. It didn't even look like a string.

She gave Jet a liver treat and uncoiled the yarn, just a little. Jet accepted the snack and kept his focus on the ball. Morgan petted the dog's scruff—his coat was getting healthier and shinier now that he was eating well. He was filling out, too. Then, while Jet stared at the ball, Morgan tied the yarn loosely around his collar and kept the other end in her hand. Holding the ball out in front of her like a dangled carrot, she held her breath and started to walk. Jet walked with her!

All Jet could think about was Ball. Ball! Ball! Ball! He loved Ball. He loved chasing Ball. He loved just looking at Ball! He followed Morgan (she had Ball!) all around the training grounds, waiting for her to throw it again. They walked in a big circle. Then they walked in a small circle.

Morgan let out a giggle. Her idea was working!

Jet heard the laugh and looked up at the girl. Out of the corner of his eye he saw something. It was long like the choker leash. It was thin like the choker leash. It was attached to his collar! Jet's throat tightened. He started to shake. He wanted to run. He had to get away from the choker before he was trapped! But . . .

Morgan stopped. Jet stopped. The choker was *not*

choking. Jet sat. Morgan offered him a treat. This choker was light. It didn't pull.

"Good dog, Jet," Morgan praised him. Jet stopped quivering. He stopped thinking about the choker. He had other things to think about. Good things. Like Ball. And treats. And Morgan. And Ball!

13

Morgan leaped off the school bus and raced toward the welcome center at Sterling ranch.

"Hey, what's your hurry?" Juniper shouted at her rapidly retreating back.

Morgan didn't reply—she was too excited. She'd managed to get all her homework done during study hall and lunch and was 100 percent free to train Jet . . . as soon as she showed her mom that her work was complete. Huffing and puffing, she found Georgia in her side office in the center and laid her work across the tidy but paper-strewn desk.

"Hi, Morgan," her mother half joked. "How was your day?"

Morgan rocked back and forth from her heels to her toes and grinned. "Good, but it's about to get better!" she replied.

Shaking her head in bemusement, Georgia lifted her daughter's handouts and notebook and took her time looking over her work, nodding as she did so. "Impressive, Morgan," she murmured as she examined her math problems and the beginning of a history assignment that wasn't due until later in the week. She glanced up at Morgan's eager face before continuing. "But let's not start rushing through our work just to get it done, okay?" she added pointedly. "Jet or no Jet, school comes first."

Morgan nibbled her lower lip, feeling guilty. The truth was, she did rush a little. But she also got everything done, which was what she'd agreed to. "Understood," she finally said in reply, just as Forrest and Juniper, who was already clutching Twig in one arm and Bud in the other, appeared in the doorway.

"I'm going to go help Dad work on the rubble pile," Forrest announced. The ginormous heap of construction rubble—old pipes and concrete and wood and Sheetrock and everything else that went into the construction of roads, parks, and buildings—had to be shifted regularly so that it was new to the dogs practicing their searches and agility on it. It was meant to mimic the destruction the dogs might one day face when searching for survivors after an earthquake or other disaster. Martin was constantly adding to and moving the debris around. Forrest loved to help. Especially when it involved driving the skid loader.

Georgia gave her only son a look. "Um, as soon as I finish my homework," he added, getting the silent message. Feeling lucky that her work was already finished, Morgan scooted past her siblings.

"Hi, Grandma," she said to Frances, who was answering the phones until Shelby, who stayed late on Wednesdays, got home from school.

"Afternoon, Morgan." Frances nodded, giving her granddaughter a wink as she dashed off to the canine pavilion.

Jet was already wagging when Morgan pushed

open the door, as if he knew she was coming. Morgan was fully aware that he probably *did* know—dogs could literally smell people miles away, and also had a sixth sense. Plus, they were about a hundred times smarter than most people gave them credit for.

"Hey, boy!" Morgan called as she pulled a thin rope off a hook. Since the first string test almost two weeks ago, she'd been increasing the thickness of the leads. At this point they were up to a line of rope a little more than an eighth of an inch thick. And though he cared mostly about his ball, the treats were helping, too, so she stuffed a big handful into her pocket and opened the latch to the kennel.

Jet had stopped wagging and, though he'd gotten to his feet, was hesitating a couple of feet from the door. He didn't look directly at Morgan, either.

Morgan felt a familiar flash of concern. They didn't have a lot of time, and she couldn't always see his progress clearly. Sometimes he seemed to be doing great, and other times he seemed to be regressing. It was confusing! And the worst part was that Jet was probably picking up on her worry, when rule number one in dog training was to remain calm and positive at all times!

Morgan took a breath and focused on the fact that he wasn't cowering or retreating to his corner.

"Good boy," she told him, holding out a treat. He walked up to her and gently took the nugget from her hand. "Super-good boy," she added as she slipped the loop around his collar and gave him a scratch behind the ears.

Jet chewed and swallowed and felt his tail rise a little. He still didn't like having something attached to his collar—the memories of being tied up always came flooding back. But now it didn't hurt. And most of the time he also remembered that Morgan was not like the mom or the boy. She never yelled. She never teased or forgot to feed him. Plus, Morgan was gentle. She didn't try to stare into his eyes. And most importantly, she never tied him up and left him. Whenever Morgan tied something to his collar she took him *with* her . . . everywhere she went!

"Let's get to work," she said as she crossed the pavilion to get the hose so she could fill all the dog bowls in the kennels with fresh water. Jet *loved* the hose and feeling the water under his paws whenever it dripped. Sometimes he stomped in the puddles and let the water get on his belly fur. Sometimes he took drinks from the pools on the floor. Water was almost as fun as Ball, and he was sad that filling the bowls didn't take longer. But when Morgan got out the brushes he felt better . . . grooming the other dogs was fun, too! He panted a little, wondering which dogs were going to be groomed today. He hoped one of them was . . .

"You're up again today, Pancho," Morgan said. Pancho was a giant pup who clearly had some Newfoundland in his genes. His long black-and-brown fur needed regular brushing to keep it from matting together.

"Arf!" Jet agreed. Pancho was big and smelly and friendly. Today they were just brushing—he'd been washed the day before. They brought him over to the grooming mat in the corner and got to work.

"You're a gentle giant, aren't you, Pancho?" Morgan cooed as she started on the fur under his neck. Pancho had deceptively strong muscles under his thick coat. While Morgan brushed, Jet got to work sniffing his hindquarters, which took a while because there was a lot of ground to cover.

"Time to swap, Jet," Morgan singsonged. When Jet was alongside her like this and they were doing chores, she felt happy and content. She stood and stretched. Jet stood, too, stretched his front legs, and got his butt waaayyy up in the air before resettling near Poncho's head. He had his own grooming to do on the big guy's neck and ears. Poncho sniffed Jet's head in a leisurely manner, waiting patiently for the grooming to be finished.

"Okay, I think you're done!" Morgan said. Jet got to his feet and led Pancho back to his kennel. He was ready to get outside. He was ready for Ball!

Morgan chuckled as she noticed Jet eyeing her. She knew what he was waiting for. When she pulled a tennis ball out of the toy basket, his eyes widened in excitement and he gave a little leap in the air.

"Sit, Jet," she told him. His eyes still riveted, he lowered his rear to the ground. "Good boy," she said. "Now, let's go."

Out on the training grounds, Roxanne and the new training hire, Eloise, were hard at work doing "find" commands with a German shepherd mix named Phoenix. Phoenix had a long, tapered snout and was playful and vocal. Since he was pretty new to the ranch and it was early in his training, Eloise wasn't hiding very far away. Phoenix was also using a scent pad—a patch of ground that was laced with Eloise's signature smell as well as one of Eloise's T-shirts—to get her scent well into his snout. Roxanne released Phoenix to find Eloise a moment before Morgan and Jet appeared on the pathway.

The pair were headed farther out on the ranch where Morgan had been putting Jet through his paces near Pedro's trailer. Roxanne knew her attention should have been on Phoenix, but she took a moment to watch Jet. She was curious about how Morgan's work with him was going. The border collie was doing a good job walking alongside the girl—he appeared calm and obedient. And Roxanne had to give Morgan credit for her outside-the-box anti-fear training.

The string approach wasn't something she would have considered, but it was clearly working. Their progress together was obvious. And yet there was something about the pup's body language that worried the lead trainer. It wouldn't have been evident to someone with a less knowledgeable eye, but she had years of experience with all kinds of breeds and rescues. The way Jet was carrying himself spoke volumes: The new dog's tail drooped a bit, his back was hunched, and his eyes were constantly roving. As she watched the two walk away she let out a slow sigh. Though there had been improvements, and Morgan still had time, there was no denying it: Jet's body language still revealed plenty of fear and uncertainty, which was making Roxanne experience fear and uncertainty of her own—fear that Jet might never make it as a rescue dog.

14

Morgan led Jet out of the pavilion and onto the training grounds, which were empty. She'd set it up this way on purpose. Now that they were hard at work on obedience, Morgan wanted a more official training space and zero audience members.

Jet's lead was two sizes thicker—closing in on a quarter inch. And just now, when she went to let him out of his kennel, he'd approached her quickly, and was only a bit crouched. Things were going well.

"Okay, lesson number six," Morgan said as she came to a halt near the center of the large empty space. "Heel," in particular, had been easy for Jet to master. Morgan guessed that this was because he'd been heeling every afternoon when they walked around tied together!

She looked down at the border collie, and he looked down, too. "Sit," she said.

Jet quickly planted his rump on the ground. These sessions were not as fun as Ball—not by a long shot! But once he learned what each command meant, he didn't mind doing what Morgan asked. He enjoyed knowing how the games worked, and there were treats . . . sometimes even Ball after he'd done well!

Jet appreciated Morgan more and more. She came to get him every day, and always told him he was a good dog. Still, he had whispering doubts inside. There was no way for him to know for sure that Morgan would *always* be there. She could forget him. She could leave him. She could decide he wasn't worth the trouble. That he didn't deserve her care. That's what happened with the boy, wasn't it? One day he liked him, and was nice. And then one day he didn't.

Jet didn't want to see in Morgan's eyes the mean look the boy got after he stopped caring—not ever—and he worked extra hard to please her.

"Good sit," Morgan praised Jet, gave him a treat, and moved on to "down." Then they practiced "stay," which was a little confusing at first. Up to that point he had followed Morgan everywhere, and now she wanted him to lie down and watch her go! Eventually he understood, though "stay" was easier when Morgan wasn't holding Ball.

Ball came out again when they were working on "leave it." Leaving Ball felt impossible at first. It took the two of them an entire session to get Jet to leave Ball a single time. And it was really, really hard. But, Jet learned, if he could force himself to leave Ball for several seconds, he would get rewarded with two throws. And since Morgan threw Ball far, he always got a good run and chase.

Today Jet held himself back the very first time Morgan told him to "leave it," and Morgan rewarded him with three throws! Jet leaped after Ball. He caught up to it on a bounce and snatched it out of the air. He loved feeling the breeze in his fur and his paws hitting the ground firmly as he ran. Ball was the *best*! But after the three throws it was back to work—and on something new: "come."

Morgan unclipped the tether and asked Jet to sit. "Stay," she told him when he was settled. She held her hand in front of his face, palm out, and then walked away. Jet squirmed a little. He didn't like it when she walked away from him! But she didn't go far, and called him to her as soon as she turned around. "Come!"

Jet was all too happy to return to Morgan's side. He trotted up to her and stood close. They practiced this several times, and every time Jet felt a pang of worry when she walked away, and relief when she called him back to her. She walked farther and farther, stretching the distance between them. Jet didn't like it but forced himself to stay until she told him to come.

"Come, Jet!" Jet ran to her, tongue out at first, and then pulled it back in, slowing for his final steps to her. Watching his approach, Morgan felt a pang of worry—a worry that had been building over the past week. In spite of all the improvements Jet had made, he wasn't looking her directly in the eye. He never had.

It seemed normal enough at first for a dog with his traumatic past to avoid eye contact. But they'd been together every day now for weeks, and for the last several days she'd been trying to get him to look directly at her in several different scenarios. In the kennel, while they played ball, during the outdoor training sessions. She'd tried to be casual about it so it wouldn't seem confrontational, but it didn't seem to matter. Jet had not met her gaze directly. Not even once.

Jet trotted slowly back to Morgan, who was standing in the shade of a big oak tree. After too much sun exposure as a young pup, Jet liked shade almost as much as he liked water! But as he approached Morgan, he got a nervous feeling. Morgan was doing something different lately, and today more than ever. She was looking at him . . . at his face . . . She was trying to look in his eyes.

Part of him wanted to look back at her, but another part didn't. Another part was afraid of what he might see in her eyes. What if they got narrow and mean the way the boy's had?

So Jet watched the ground under his paws, like he always did, as he approached. He sat down at her feet. He peeked up at her face without looking into her eyes and quickly glanced away.

"Look!" Morgan said calmly and firmly in what she thought of as her training voice. Jet had never heard the "look" command before. Morgan held a treat in front of her face. And not just any treat, either. This was something new. Something meaty. Jet sniffed the air. He drooled.

"Look!" Morgan repeated. "You like hot dogs?" she asked.

Jet had never had a hot dog. But he wanted it! It smelled delicious! He licked his chops.

He looked at the treat.

"Look," Morgan said the word again. "Look at me." She was practically begging. She needed him to do this one thing or he'd never be okayed for

117

SAR training, and Morgan would probably *never* be asked to evaluate another dog. "I know you can do this, Jet," she whispered. "You have to."

Jet looked at the edge of her fingers, close to her eyes. He could feel her eyes locked on his. He felt nervous. He couldn't look directly back at her. When he lived in the yard, he looked in the boy's eyes all the time. He searched them for signs of kindness, which he rarely saw. Sometimes the boy would hold out food and Jet would look into his eyes to ask if he could please have some of it. The boy would hold it closer. His eyes would say yes. But then his eyes would narrow and he'd laugh the mean laugh and take the food away. The boy's eyes were unkind. They lied. So Jet stopped looking. He stopped looking at the boy. He stopped looking at everyone. And he'd been afraid to look ever since.

Morgan tried a second time, and a third.

When he still couldn't look her in the eye, Morgan asked him to do one of the commands he'd already mastered, and then gave him the hot dog. She didn't withhold food. Training was all about rewards—not punishment. It was possible that Jet didn't even understand what she was asking for . . . Eye contact wasn't easy to explain to a dog, especially a dog who wasn't accustomed to making it! But it was so essential. Without it Jet would never be able to really communicate with his handler on a rescue. If Jet couldn't "look," his training would be over before it ever really started.

15

"Pass the mashed potatoes," Forrest said, eyeing the steaming bowl hungrily from his seat at the table. Georgia passed him a stern look instead until he added a sheepish "please." The entire Sterling Center clan was gathered around the large table—including Frances Sterling, Pedro, and Roxanne. This was routine on Thursdays, but today was Tuesday . . . which meant that there would probably be a second group meal on Thursday. Forrest loved these big dinners because there was even more food than usual. Plus it was always great for everyone to catch up on ranch news in a festive—and delicious—atmosphere.

"Save some for the rest of us," Shelby groused, watching her only brother build a giant white pile on his plate.

Forrest made a face and passed the bowl along. They all knew that Georgia made tons of mashed potatoes. They were everyone's favorite. The same was true of her roast veggies and chicken. With gravy, of course.

Morgan piled her plate high, too, before digging in. As usual, the chicken was tender and juicy and the veggies roasted to sweet perfection. Everything tasted delicious, and she felt happy to have everyone around her. Plus, Jet hadn't needed to be coaxed to the kennel door at all today—he cheerfully trotted over on his own! They'd had a great training session, and his prey drive was as strong as ever. He was really on his way—at least that was what she was repeating in her head in order to drown out her worry.

"How's the training going with Jet?" Martin asked, shooting Juniper a look to make sure she heard the dog's name. Otherwise they'd get another earful about cat training!

"Good!" Morgan replied, wondering if her dad could hear the worry in her voice as loudly as she did. She smiled and looked at her grandmother instead.

Frances's blue eyes sparkled from across the table, and she nodded approvingly. Though Frances was retired from managing the ranch's day-to-day operations, she was happy to hear all the news and still felt enormous pride at seeing how seamlessly her son and daughter-in-law had taken over. She knew the easy transition was due in part to her grandchildren, who had taken to the dogs as wholeheartedly as their parents had . . . with the exception of Juniper, of course. And though it was Forrest who shared her blue eyes and spunky personality, she saw herself most clearly in Morgan. The two had a shared passion for dog training as well as a seemingly unquenchable thirst for knowledge. At eleven, Morgan knew more than some of the adult trainers Frances had hired back in the day, and she'd always been a bit of a stickler!

"I'm glad to hear it, Morgan," Pedro said, helping

himself to more chicken. "Jet has real potential."

Georgia cleared her throat. Morgan thought she was going to say something about Jet, but her mother had her eyes on Shelby. "No phones at the table," she reminded the high schooler.

"Are you texting Rye-annn?" Juniper asked in singsong. Ryan Westerly and Shelby had been going out for several months in spite of a rocky start and the boy's significant dog allergy.

Shelby hit send, shot her littlest sister a major glare, and set her phone on the sideboard behind her. "Sorry, Mom."

"Pedro, do you want to hear about *my* training?" Juniper piped up. "Because I'm one hundred and fifty percent sure that Jet couldn't use a toilet like my kitties if his life depended on it."

"Your cats are using a toilet . . . a human toilet?" Frances asked, aghast. She'd never heard of such a thing, though she also wouldn't put it past her youngest granddaughter to try something so outrageous.

"Yes!" Juniper crowed.

While everyone smiled at her ridiculous but highly persistent cat cheerleading, Roxanne turned to Morgan, who was sitting beside her. "Is Jet making any eye contact?" she asked quietly. Morgan swallowed her bite of chicken, feeling a wave of alarm. Leave it to Roxanne to put her finger on exactly what was worrying her!

"Not yet," she half mumbled. Part of her didn't want to talk about this in front of everyone. But another part knew they were a team, and that sharing information often led to solutions. Hadn't she been comforted by everyone being together just a few minutes ago? Besides, there was no point in trying to keep secrets in this crowd.

Morgan took a sip of water and a slow breath before answering. "I wasn't pressuring him in the beginning because he was so vulnerable. I didn't want to challenge him, you know? I think he trusts me now . . . mostly. But, honestly, no. He still won't look me in the eye."

Roxanne nodded. "I was afraid of that." She felt for Morgan, but she had to be clear and honest.

And realistic. As head trainer that was her job. "Eye contact is a really important display of trust," she said. "If Jet isn't able to make eye contact with a partner, there won't be a partnership . . ."

From across the table, Pedro was chewing and nodding, too. "It's impossible to communicate with a dog who won't look at you," he said after he'd swallowed. "Ideally, a dog and his handler can have whole conversations with eye contact alone." He'd seen it with many pairs. No trust, no communication. Though nobody said his name, Morgan sensed that they were all suddenly thinking of Race.

For a long minute, the only sound in the dining room was chewing and clinking forks.

Roxanne leaned back in her chair. She gathered everything Morgan had told her along with her own observations and mulled them over in her head. Jet was still having significant issues, but they were also midstream in the process. They had time, and a possible opportunity. Morgan and Jet had both been working hard. The whole team had to be committed to make the most of it. Morgan needed to know that she was behind her—that they all were—if she and Jet were going to have a shot.

"Do you want me to come and work with you tomorrow?" Roxanne asked. "Maybe if I spend some time and see exactly what's going on I can help clarify things and possibly give you some pointers."

Pedro's head tilted to the side . . . He was thinking. "I have some time tomorrow afternoon to help, too," he offered.

Morgan felt a wave of relief. The dream team was in the house and on her side! And though she had agreed—begged—to take Jet on to get him to a place where he could enter search and rescue training, the Sterling crew was a squad and worked best when they worked together. She didn't have to do this totally alone. She could accept help. And she needed it!

"That would be great," she said. "Thanks," she added. She felt hopeful again. Hopeful, and happy she'd told them all the truth!

16

Morgan stared out the window of the school bus, lost in thought. She'd been distracted all day, trying to think of how she might be able to get Jet to make eye contact with her. She'd actually written "Jet" instead of her own name in the top corner of her vocabulary quiz, and Mrs. Leachmeer had to call her up to her desk to make sure it was hers. It was so embarrassing!

Even after a whole day of obsessing and being distracted, Morgan hadn't come up with any genius ideas. Now, as she rode the bus home, she was working hard not to dwell on what would happen if she couldn't get the sweet pup to look her in the eye and instead focus on finishing her homework so she could get right to training. She wrote several answers in her English packet. Then she found herself staring out the window again. It was just that Jet had so much potential! And it seemed like he trusted her except for this one tiny thing, which was really actually huge. Morgan's stomach knotted, and she reminded herself that at least today she would have help.

She thought back to dinner the night before and the looks she'd seen passing between Roxanne and Pedro across the table—the two of them certainly made eye contact easily! She knew what they had been telegraphing back and forth with their glances. Concern. Worry, even. Morgan was worried, too.

"You coming?" Forrest prodded his sister's shoulder as the bus pulled to a halt in front of the ranch.

"Oh!" Morgan started. "Thanks." She grabbed her backpack and followed her brother and sister off the bus, homework still in hand. She walked slowly behind them to the welcome center for the usual after-school check-in ritual with their mom. Inside, Shelby, who got a ride home from high school, was already at the desk handling the phones. Working at the center was Shelby's after-school job. When she was at school or off being a teenager, front-desk duty fell to Georgia or Frances. But Georgia dashed to the back office to crunch numbers and handle the behind-the-scenes business whenever the welcome desk was covered.

Shelby hung up the phone and made a note on a pad of paper before looking up at her sisters and brother. She saw the papers in Morgan's hand. "I can check your homework!" she offered while Juniper and Forrest pushed past Morgan to talk to their mom.

Morgan paused. Having her older sister look over her work could be a good thing or a bad thing depending on Shelby's mood. Morgan considered while Shelby inspected her nails. Shel had been pretty cheerful lately. She hadn't griped at her when she left her clothes on the floor in a heap or yelled when she'd accidentally woken her up before her alarm went off that morning. And Forrest and Juniper were going to be a minute with their mom. All in all it was worth the risk.

"Thanks." Morgan handed over her English packet, and Shelby took her time reading through the pages before writing a big smiley face on the top.

"Shelby!" Morgan moaned. "I'm not in kindergarten!"

Shelby giggled while Morgan fretted about what Mrs. Leachmeer would think when she saw the ridiculous face. "Thanks!" Morgan grumbled half sarcastically.

When her mom's office had cleared of Sterling siblings, Morgan stepped inside to show her mom that her homework had been checked. Georgia had the phone pressed to an ear, but gave her a little smile and a thumbs-up. She had the all clear.

After dropping her school stuff off at the house, Morgan found herself walking extremely slowly to the pavilion. One part of her was anxious to get to work. Another part of her was just anxious. She knew she needed Roxanne's and Pedro's help, and was grateful, but what if they saw something going on with the border collie that was worse than she thought? Or what if her approach was all wrong? What if the lack of eye contact was her fault? Her stomach knotted up at the thought—the pain in her gut was becoming all too familiar. More ugh.

Inside the pavilion, Jet was dozing on his bed and dreaming about running. His legs twitched as he chased Ball across a field, over a fence, and into the woods. Ball kept going and going, and so did Jet. When the pavilion door opened, he jerked awake. The only thing better than dream Ball was real Ball! By the time Morgan unlatched his kennel door Jet was on his feet and waiting.

"Hey, boy," she said, trying to catch his eye and also *not* catch his eye at the same time. She told herself that it was good that he was waiting at the door—he'd only done that a couple of times, and it was a recent development. Progress!

Outside, Roxanne was at the training grounds with the German shepherd mix Phoenix, who was wagging his tail and sniffing a patch of grass.

"Oh, good, you're here," she called out to Morgan. "Phoenix and I have been waiting."

"We're working the dogs together?" Morgan couldn't keep the surprise out of her voice. She liked Phoenix a lot, but had expected that they'd just be working with Jet.

Roxanne tucked a strand of hair that had come loose from her ponytail behind her ear. "I want you to see the two dogs side by side," she explained. "Before we get to work on possible solutions, I want to show you what Jet's body language and behavior are revealing. Every dog is different, but some things are universal. I want you to see what I'm concerned about."

Morgan reached down instinctively to give Jet a pat. Roxanne's plan made a lot of sense but wasn't exactly reassuring. The trainer wanted to see what was wrong, while Morgan wanted to focus on making it right!

A few minutes later Pedro arrived, and they got down to canine body language business. Roxanne put the dogs through a few simple exercises—exactly the kinds of obedience skills Morgan had been working on with Jet. Their weeks of work together paid off, too. Jet matched Phoenix easily on "sit," "stay," "heel," "come," and even "leave it." He heeled on leash as if he wasn't tethered at all!

"Wow, you've really trained him well," Pedro said, stroking his salt-and-pepper goatee. Morgan felt a flash of satisfaction.

"He's a smart dog," Roxanne added. "And he learns quickly."

Morgan sensed that the "but" was coming and braced herself. But instead of saying anything else, Roxanne simply handed Phoenix's lead to Morgan so she was only holding Jet's.

Jet looked up at the tall, speckled lady. She wasn't Morgan, but she smelled like dog—dog fur and dog drool and general dogginess. He liked her!

"Sit, Jet," she told him. Jet sat. "Down, Jet." Jet lay down. He liked this game, even though Phoenix wasn't playing it with him anymore. He liked it when he knew what do to. "Stay," Roxanne said. She held her palm in front of his face. It smelled like dog treats, but Jet stopped himself from licking it. Work time was not licking time. "Stay," she said again.

Jet watched Roxanne walk away from him. He waited and tried to stay still. She walked and walked and walked. Finally she turned around.

"Come, Jet," she called.

Jet got to his feet and started toward her in one smooth motion. He ran, feeling the wind in his fur and letting his tongue loll just a little bit. But as he got closer, he realized she was looking right at him. He sensed it before he saw it and instinctually dipped his head to avoid her gaze. He wanted to look but something wouldn't let him. Something deep inside told him, "Don't look don't look don't look!"

The feeling made Jet feel bad. Like a bad dog. His tail and ears dropped, and his run turned into a slow slink as he got close to the freckled lady who smelled so good.

Roxanne sighed. She couldn't have asked for a better demonstration of non-trusting dog body language, but she'd hoped that Jet would prove her wrong—that he would take this essential step with her . . . or at least not make it obvious that he was far from it. She almost didn't want to put Phoenix through the same exercise because it felt like rubbing salt into a wound to compare the two. And yet she needed to be sure that Morgan understood.

Phoenix, on release from the "down stay," was 100 percent happy dog exuberance. He held his head high, making sure to catch *everyone's* eye. He flashed each and every one of them a big doggy grin and stared up into Roxanne's face waiting for the next command.

The difference was not lost on Morgan, who bit her lip in distress. Jet had talent to be sure. He also had issues.

"That's the difference between a dog with confidence—a dog who can trust—and one who can't," Roxanne said, making an effort to be gentle and honest at the same time. She was still having her doubts about Jet. She wanted it all to work out, but she wanted Morgan to be prepared to let go if it didn't.

"Are there any tricks for making a dog trust you?" Morgan asked.

"Tricks, no. Just time," Roxanne said. "Time, patience, and consistency."

Pedro and Roxanne shared a look, and Pedro added, "And sometimes all the time in the world isn't enough. Some dogs never get to a place where they can trust. They're too broken. We don't know exactly what Jet has been through, or what impact his past has on him. It might not be something he can recover from."

"My best advice is to keep doing what you've been doing. Be there. Be consistent," Roxanne said, and then added, "he's come a long way thanks to your good work. If I were a dog who didn't trust I'd be glad to be in your hands, Morgan. But that doesn't mean you can control the outcome. You can only do your best."

Pedro was nodding. "Time will tell."

Time. The one thing that was seriously limited. Morgan knew that she was nearly four weeks into the five weeks she'd been granted, which meant she only had a little over a week left. Nine days, to be precise. It wasn't much.

"Thanks for your help," she told Roxanne and Pedro as she took Jet's lead and headed back to the pavilion. Nine days. She had nine days. Her feet felt heavy and her body leaden. With each pounding step she tried to strengthen her resolve. Her hands curled into fists. She'd make the most of every day, every session, every minute. Before she put Jet back into his kennel she crouched down, closed her eyes, and touched her forehead to his. "We can do this, boy, I know it."

Jet didn't know what she was saying, but he gave her a lick to show her that he knew it was important.

17

Morgan's eyelids felt like they were made of concrete—scratchy and heavy. Mrs. Leachmeer was at the front of the room talking to the kids about sentence structure to review for an end-of-the-school-year test. Morgan could tell because she saw her write a diagram on the board, and because her teacher's lips were moving. But she was unable to make out what she was saying. She blinked. And blinked again. Each time it got harder to reopen her eyes.

"Stay!" Morgan jerked awake, swiping her bare forearm through a pool of drool on her desk. Reaching out her other hand to wipe it, she half shook her head in horror. Did she really just shout

out a dog-training command in her sleep . . . during English?

The rest of the class guffawed while her face
grew hot.

"No, sit!" a boy behind her crowed.

"Stay . . . awake?" Mrs. Leachmeer asked with a
sly smile. Her teacher knew about the family business and had visited the Sterling Center more than
once. She was a dog person herself and had already
guessed that Morgan was obsessing about a dog
named Jet—so much that she had substituted his
name for her own.

"Let's get started on our diagraming review," she
instructed the class as she approached Morgan's
desk. "Dreaming about dogs?" she asked quietly,
crouching down. "You seem tired, Morgan. Is everything okay?"

"Yes . . . I mean no . . . I mean yes." She wasn't
sure how to answer that question!

Mrs. Leachmeer patted her arm. "Try to stay
focused on school right now, all right? We only have
a few more days!"

Morgan nodded as her teacher went back to her desk. The boy behind her was still chuckling and Morgan was still embarrassed, but also grateful Mrs. Leachmeer understood, and was letting her off easy.

Morgan opened to the right page and tried to read the review questions. The words swam before her eyes. She was so tired! She'd been up at five thirty every morning for the last week and a half. Besides that, she'd been so anxious she hadn't slept well to begin with! And now here it was, the five-week mark. The time period she'd been granted to get Jet ready to start search and rescue training would be over in a few short hours. And Jet? He'd continued to make progress but still wasn't making eye contact.

Morgan blinked, realizing that the words were blurring now because she was tearing up. She loved Jet so much! Most of his skills were off the charts, which made his lack of trust especially heart-breaking. He could be the best candidate in every possible way, but none of it mattered if he was incapable of trust.

The hardest part was that Morgan felt in her bones that he *did* trust her . . . most of the time. And Roxanne and Pedro, who had come to watch them work together several times in the past week plus, told her over and over that she was doing everything right. That Jet's issues were not her fault. That some dogs couldn't overcome their traumatic pasts enough to become SAR dogs. Still, she felt responsible.

Wiping her eyes, Morgan told herself that whatever happened, Jet would still have a nice life. They would find an active person or family to love him and keep him busy. Deep inside, though, she worried that this might be easier said than done. A rescued dog with issues was hard enough to handle. Add in Jet's brains and energy, and there was just one real solution: He needed a job to keep him occupied.

The rest of the school day was a blur, though luckily Morgan managed to stay awake and get through it. By the time she got home, finished her schoolwork, and made it to the pavilion, she was a nervous wreck.

Shelby was there filling the bowl they kept in the welcome center with dog treats. The eldest Sterling took one look at her little sister and knew she was in bad shape.

"Hey," she said. "Are you heading out for Jet's evaluation?"

Morgan nodded. "Today is the day," she said. "And I don't think he's going to do it."

Shelby closed the cupboard and turned toward her sister. "You have to believe in him," she said kindly. "You have to let Jet know that *you* trust *him*."

Morgan didn't always like when her big sister gave her advice, but something about Shelby's words rang true. She'd been so worried and anxious about getting Jet to trust her that she was probably sending off untrustworthy vibes!

"And trust yourself," Shelby said. "If anyone can pull this off, it's you. You're like a dog magician, Morgan."

Morgan smiled a half smile. Compliments from Shelby were rare. She'd hang on to this one!

Shelby reached out and squeezed Morgan's arm.

"I've got to get back to the desk before Mom finds out I left for two minutes," she said. "But you've got this."

Morgan felt a bit lighter as she got Jet out of his kennel, and before taking him anywhere she squatted down in front of him and tried to look into his bicolored eyes.

"Just look at me?" she asked gently. "You trust me, don't you?"

Jet stood close, leaning slightly into Morgan. He listened to the soft timbre of her voice. He could tell that she was asking him for something . . . something big. Jet liked Morgan. He liked all the folks on the ranch. But deep under his fur was a hard, cold place, a place that never softened. A place that told him not to trust. A place that was certain he only had himself.

"I trust you," Morgan whispered in the dog's soft ear. "You got this, too."

"How's it going in here?" a voice called, interrupting the moment. It was Frances. "I came to tell you we're ready when you are."

Morgan jumped up and turned to her grand-mother. "Oh! I didn't mean to keep anyone waiting!"

"Nonsense." Frances waved a hand toward the door as she approached the kennel. "You two are what's important. The others can wait until you're good and ready." She reached a slow hand out to Jet, who sniffed it.

But Morgan had had her moment with Jet and didn't see any use in waiting. It was time. So she attached the lead to Jet's collar, which he accepted readily, and led him outside.

Roxanne, Pedro, Georgia, and Martin were on the training grounds, though not exactly waiting for her. Juniper, who had Twig and Bud on slender leashes, was giving the adults an elaborate demon-stration of her kitty training. Surprisingly, she had both cats sitting still at the same moment.

"Are those scratches on your arms, June Bug?" Martin asked.

Juniper shrugged. "I call them love scuffs."

"Well, let's make sure we wash those love scuffs

tonight before you go to sleep," Georgia said. "We don't want them turning into love scars."

"Fine," Juniper said with a small scowl. Then she broke into a big smile as she bent down to unhook Twig. Twig blinked at her slowly, as if remembering she was there at all.

"Stay," Juniper commanded. Twig blinked again and held stock-still for two seconds.

"Good kit—"

Juniper was mid-congratulations when the orange tabby bolted in the direction of the rubble pile, right past Forrest, who was jogging up to see Jet's demo.

"Twig, come!" Juniper shouted, scooping up Bud and chasing after Twig's tail, which flicked the air as he raced away.

"We're still working on recall!" Juniper, exasperated, shouted over her shoulder.

When Juniper was out of earshot, Pedro let out the laugh he'd been holding. "You think she'll ever give up on cat training?" he asked as he dabbed his eyes.

"Sure," Forrest quipped. "Right after she decides she loves dogs as much as cats."

While everyone chuckled, Morgan took one last moment to crouch next to Jet and give him some love. "You can do this, Jet," she said. "I know there is trust somewhere inside you." And with that, she led him to the center of the training grounds to begin their demonstration.

Since Jet had shown his mastery of obedience commands more than once, Morgan wasn't expected to take him through every command—she'd been told to demonstrate a few basic skills before moving on to the thing everyone was worried about . . . eye contact. But Morgan had the sense that Jet wanted to go through most of it, so that's what she did with him. She asked him to sit, lie down, and stay, and then orchestrated a "leave it." He was so good at leaving the ball now!

Jet looked at Ball on the ground. Ball! He wanted Ball! But Morgan had asked him to leave it, and he liked to do what Morgan said. So he just looked at Ball, even when Morgan asked Forrest to pick it up and throw it. Jet watched it sail through the air away from him while his back legs twitched. He didn't move, even when Forrest went after the ball to see where it had landed.

"Good 'leave it,' Jet," Morgan told him. And then, after waiting a full thirty seconds, she said, "Get it!"

Jet was gone in a flash, searching for Ball. A minute or so after the dog disappeared into the trees, Forrest returned out of breath. "There's no way he can get it," he called out as he approached. "He'd have to actually climb the tree. It's lodged in a notch too high up even for me."

"Okay, let's call him back and start over," Roxanne said.

Morgan tried not to feel rattled. This was a curve ball . . . literally! Still, she had to try.

"Come, Jet!" she called. And a few seconds later, "Jet . . . come!"

Everyone waited for the young black-and-white border collie to appear. Morgan held her breath. "Jet!" she said, letting it all out in a whoosh. He wasn't coming. She turned to Roxanne, a question in her misting eyes. What should she do now?

"There he is!" Frances hooted, pointing. Jet was sprinting toward them, and he had the tennis ball in his mouth!

Jet's ears flapped as he ran. Ball hadn't been easy to get. Ball was up high! He had to climb. But Morgan told him to get Ball, so he got Ball.

Jet could feel all the eyes on him as he raced toward Morgan. He felt their surprise, and their happiness, and their excitement. He saw Morgan and felt her pride. And her love. He felt the firmly rooted nugget of fear, too. But it felt smaller than usual—a lot smaller. And the happiness and positive energy rushing in his direction was *absolutely gigantic.*

Jet remembered how tiny he'd felt when he was tied up in the dusty yard. How nobody—not even the boy—really cared for him. But Morgan and Forrest and the speckled lady cared for him. Every day. And as Morgan watched him run toward her, her whole body looked and smelled like happiness.

Jet slowed as he approached, trotting up to her

with his tail held high. He dropped the ball at her feet, sat down next to her, and leaned his body into her calf. Riding the wave of happy coming off the people around him, he looked up, right into Morgan's eyes.

18

Morgan felt the warmth of the dog pressed up against her leg, looked into his eyes, and lapped up every second of eye contact! Even as her vision blurred with tears again—this time happy tears—she did not look away from the blue-and-brown-eyed pup. She was so happy and relieved and proud she felt like she might just float away. Jet did it! *They* did it!

Behind her, everyone watching clapped and cheered as she gave Jet his treat and dropped to her knees to nuzzle him. It might not be the most official response for the end of a successful exercise, but she was so filled with love for this amazing animal she couldn't help herself. "Oh, Jet!" she said happily. "Good dog."

Jet licked the salty tears off her cheeks. He felt bigger and stronger than he ever had in his life.

Suddenly Roxanne was beside them. "Congratulations!" She knelt down and put an arm around each of their shoulders. Jet turned his snout and licked the speckled lady's face, too.

"That was definitely trusting eye contact, Morgan. No question. He's made the shift. Your work with him has been transformational."

Morgan beamed at Jet, and then at Roxanne, and then back at Jet. She still couldn't believe it. He'd looked right at her, holding her gaze. It had felt nothing short of miraculous!

Now her family was crowded around them. Georgia squeezed her daughter's shoulders. "That was brilliant, Liebling!"

"I can't believe he got that ball," Forrest said with a shake of his head. "That thing was up in that tree . . . like at least five feet up!"

"I guess he has some tree-climbing skills we didn't know about," Martin mused.

"I've seen that before," Roxanne said, getting to her feet and stretching her long legs. "But only once; it's very unusual. Jet is definitely ready to start SAR training in earnest. I think he's going to be amazing."

Pedro was wearing a wide smile. "Increíble!" he said in his native Spanish. "He's going to need a partner with an extra-gentle touch," he added, thinking aloud. Though the trust Morgan had established was clear, it was still new and fragile. He didn't want to jeopardize it after all Morgan's—and Jet's—hard work. Pedro knew from experience that a firm but tender handler wasn't always easy to find. It could take him as long to find the right person as it would take Roxanne and Eloise and the rest of the team to get Jet through the core training . . . months!

Pedro crouched beside Jet, who looked him right in the eye before giving him a lick. "Okay." Pedro laughed. "I'm on the job."

After a celebratory pizza dinner at the Sterling house, to which Jet himself was invited, Pedro headed up to his trailer thinking hard about where he might find the right partner for a border collie with a big heart. He'd been considering this off and on, but it hadn't seriously been on his radar until this afternoon when all signals said go. He made himself a cup of tea and settled at his little dining table with a bag of chocolate chip cookies and his computer.

The center received dozens of requests every month from fire departments, ski resorts, airports, and independent SAR teams . . . all looking for potential search and rescue dogs and the opportunity to train at the Sterling Center. Though the ranch was big and well established, they couldn't accept even a quarter of the requests. And not every person they accepted became a successful match, either. Some were unable to make the necessary time commitment. Others didn't realize the hours and weeks and months of work involved. Pedro made his choices carefully, because the humans would almost always give up before the dogs. The dogs never quit! And when a human failed to follow through, it could be heartbreaking. But when it worked out? Sometimes Pedro felt more like a matchmaker than a trainer.

Pedro took a sip of tea and scrolled through the recent requests. Before long his eyes were screen weary. Still, he kept at it. He stayed at his table late into the night, reading requests and flagging possible candidates. Some sounded like they might work, but none felt exactly right. Pedro couldn't explain how he knew this—he just did. Rubbing his eyes, he sighed. Jet's skill level was off the charts, and so was his sensitivity . . .

"Maybe tomorrow," he said to no one as he reached out to close his laptop. But before he did so a subject header in an email caught his eye: HARDWORKING DOG LOVER, FIREFIGHTER, AND SAR VOLUNTEER LOOKING TO EXPAND EXPERIENCE. Pedro clicked open the email. It was from a woman in Washington State who, as stated in her subject line, was a firefighter, dog owner, and search and rescue volunteer.

There was something about the tone in her letter—experienced but also humble and a little bit cautious. Her list of rescue participation was long and included some challenging deployments. At the top of his list, Pedro put down her name and contact information. Then he printed her request for a canine partner and shut down his computer. It was nearly midnight. He'd make the call in the morning.

19

Molly O'Dell pulled her attention from the California countryside on the other side of the window and sat back in her train seat. Stretching her long legs, she lifted her long blond hair off her neck. It was hot in the passenger car, and she'd been sitting for hours. Arching her back, she looked over the tops of the seats in front of her. The man beside her didn't take his eyes off his phone, and she didn't want to ask him to stand up to let her out again. She leaned back and took a deep breath instead, hoping it would help her settle down. She glanced automatically at the area around her feet. Usually when Molly looked down, she could count on seeing two happy hound faces looking back at her. Her dogs, Munch and Sasha, went nearly everywhere she went, and she wished they were with her now. Their mere presence calmed her nerves, and Molly was a little anxious . . . for two reasons. One, she had never left Munch and Sasha for so long before. She was going to be gone for at least three weeks, much longer if things went well. She'd arranged excellent care for them, of course, but it wasn't going to be easy to be separated from them for so long.

The second reason Molly was on edge was that she was doing something completely new and challenging and wasn't at all sure how it was going to go.

She was headed to the Sterling Center to receive training as a search and rescue handler. And if it all went according to plan, she'd be coming home with a third dog—her very own canine SAR partner!

Molly sat back and closed her eyes even though she knew she wouldn't be able to sleep. She told herself that everything was going to be fine, and that no matter how it all turned out she was going to a place that was full of dogs (even if they were not hers). Truth be told, Molly preferred dogs to people almost any day of the week. She loved dogs. She needed dogs. For as long as she could remember, she'd had *at least* one dog at any given point in her life, and more often she had a whole pack. There was even a picture of her as a very young baby, before she could walk, tumbling around on the floor with a pile of puppies. Dogs made Molly feel whole. And right now, on the train without her two pups, she felt a little like a puzzle missing a piece . . . or two.

The invitation from Pedro Sundal had been very specific, though. No outside dogs were allowed to be on the ranch. She had to leave Sasha and Munch behind in order to make bonding with a new dog possible. She had to arrive alone.

It had seemed to Molly that Sasha and Munch should also get a chance to meet any potential new pack members and give their sniff of approval, and she'd even emailed Mr. Sundal about it. He'd written back with an explanation that made sense even if it was hard to swallow: *The relationship you'll be building with a working dog is different from the relationship you have with your pets. I'm sure you and your dogs are very close, but a working relationship is something more. In the beginning your SAR dog—your partner—must be your primary and only focus.*

Molly tried to imagine what the bond between partners on a SAR team was like. Despite a long history with all kinds of dogs, she'd never had or lived or worked with a working dog. She'd seen a lot of impressive videos, though, and had gotten to know human-dog teams working with the local search and rescue volunteers. It was seeing those teams in action that really inspired her. The partners had a deeper level of communication than she had with her dogs—the pairs worked as singular units. She wanted to experience that and be part of the good it could do. She wanted to put all her dog sense to work for others. And the big fat bonus would be having a new dog to love!

It had seemed like a great idea when she wrote to the center. She'd felt certain then. But now, as the train chugged south, her worries bubbled to the surface. Was she really up for the task? Could she be commanding enough? She and her dogs got along wonderfully, but she tended to let Munch and Sasha rule the roost. She disliked correcting them. Would she be able to muster up the firmness required to partner with a SAR dog? Molly took a deep breath and let it out in a slow, steady stream. She was about to find out.

At the train station, Martin was already waiting in the large lobby. He peered through the arched wooden doorway and tapped his foot on the stone floor. He didn't bother to hide his smile. Meeting the people who came to the ranch, whether it was to observe, train, teach, or simply visit, was a favorite part of his job. He also loved managing and maintaining the facilities on the ranch—his main task—but each time he brought someone to Sterling Center for the first time he had the chance to see it through their eyes. It made his heart swell with pride to share what his mom had built, what he and his wife and children continued to carry forward.

And it was all in the service of dogs serving people serving dogs—a continuous loop.

Martin stepped out onto the platform to see if he could spot the train, his smile widening when he saw a metallic gleam far down the rails. Yep, he'd be meeting the new handler very soon! In his mind dog people were almost as good as the dogs themselves, and just like the dogs, each and every one was different.

The train pulled in and Martin held up the sign Shelby had made for these occasions. It was large and rigid and said STERLING CENTER in bold black type below a red circle with a dog silhouetted inside it. The new recruit wouldn't be able to miss it.

Molly's large duffel bumped the backs of her legs as she walked down the train steps. She spotted the lanky man—his blond-turning-white hair was visible over the heads of the rest of the pickup crowd—before she was close enough to read the sign. It had to be Martin Sterling! He seemed to recognize her, too, and grinned. His blue eyes twinkled.

If he'd had a tail, it would have been wagging a friendly greeting.

Molly pointed at the sign as she got closer. "You must be Martin!"

"And you must be Molly!" The two shook hands, and Martin took one strap of the giant duffel and led Molly to the car. The moment they pulled out of the lot, he began to fill Molly in on what to expect.

"You'll have your own room, of course. There's a shared bathroom down the hall and showers right across from that. There will be two other handlers training with you. They arrived yesterday. Seems like a nice bunch." Martin smiled to show Molly he was including her in that statement, too.

"You'll mostly be responsible for making your own meals—the kitchen in the handlers' lodge is stocked. You'll have group dinners twice a week, and you'll work with Pedro every day. He'll start off with classroom lessons, and after that you'll work directly with the dogs and Roxanne Valentine, our canine trainer."

Molly listened as Martin told her all about the ranch and the way things worked, feeling a wave of excitement when he mentioned the dogs. That was the part Molly was waiting for! She was dying to know when she would get to meet her dog partner. She knew pairing was important, and there was no guarantee she would find the right pooch this time. Still, she was a little desperate to meet her new pup. She so wanted this to work!

Martin steered the car around another swooping turn, and suddenly the Sterling Center came into view. Molly's mouth dropped open. She'd known the center was big and beautiful, but in person it was stunning.

A carved wood-and-stone arch spanned the entrance to the parking lot. Beyond that, large low buildings nestled among sprawling California oaks and tall evergreens. Martin pointed out the roofs and porches of major buildings that were visible from the welcome center parking lot.

"There are more buildings and more training areas we can't see from here," he explained. "We have several mock disaster areas that we use to get the dogs ready for certification and deployment, and we're always constructing more."

As she listened, Molly realized that she was half holding her breath. There was so much to explore!

Martin saw the excitement in Molly's brown eyes . . . and also noticed that she looked down frequently. He'd seen this before—she was probably looking for the dogs she'd left at home.

Martin hefted the huge duffel onto his shoulder and closed the car just as a young boy rushed out of the welcome center. The boy had black hair and brown skin, darker than his father's, but there was no doubt in Molly's mind that he was one of the Sterling kids. He moved like his dad and had the same reassuring smile and blue eyes.

"I'm Forrest," he said, sticking out his hand. He looked like he was in middle school but was already as tall as Molly. "I can give you a tour if you'd like!" he offered.

"I can take your bag to your room—you might want to start with the canine pavilion so you can see the dogs," Martin suggested. Molly laughed. Was it that obvious she was missing her best fur friends?

She looked around her feet again, searching for Sasha's lolling tongue or Munch's goofy dog grin. Just seeing either of them for a split second would calm her fizzy, anxious feelings.

"Thank you so much for the offer, guys, but I think I want to settle in a little first. It's been a long day. I'm just a bit overwhelmed." Molly took the bag from Martin and thanked him for the ride.

"Of course!" Martin said with a warm smile.

Hoisting her bag, Molly started up the path to the handlers' lodge and found room A, trying to ignore the fact that there were no paw steps following her. For the first time in ages, she would have to handle the pressure and anticipation of a new situation on her own.

20

The alarm on Molly's phone chirped, and she slowly opened her eyes. It had already been a week, and though she generally felt at home on the ranch, she simply couldn't get used to waking up to an alarm. Sasha, who was part German shepherd, part chow, part mystery, and 100 percent goofball, had been waking her up every morning for the last seven years by placing a paw on her pillow and staring at her until she opened her eyes. And on the rare occasions that the paw and stare weren't enough, Sasha would jump on the bed and lick Molly's face until she was smothered by dog kisses!

"I hear you!" Molly mumbled at her phone. She

threw the covers aside and stumbled to the other side of the room to turn it off. Sure, the phone alarm was reliable, but she liked the dog alarm better despite the fact that Sasha's morning breath was near deadly.

Within a few short minutes, Molly was dressed and ready for the day. She headed out to the common area where Richard and Victoria, her fellow handlers, were already at the table eating breakfast. Molly slid onto a seat across from them and filled a bowl with granola and fruit and yogurt.

"Coffee?" Victoria asked, lifting the carafe.

Molly nodded gratefully. She'd be almost as lost without her daily cup of joe as she was without her pups! She added a bit of milk and took a much-needed sip . . . class started in less than half an hour.

Classes with Pedro had been going well. Molly had always liked school and had always been good at it. Handler training was no different. She easily digested the important principles of dog training, discipline, and canine first aid and the science of air scenting.

Victoria, a firefighter from Maine, was less enthusiastic about the classwork. At least twice a day, she would run her hand over her pixie cut and ask Pedro in a teasing voice when they were going to get to work with dogs instead of pencils. Pedro's response was always a crooked smile and a "not yet."

Richard was older and less impatient than Victoria, but far more rigid. He took *everything* seriously. After seven days Molly didn't think she'd seen even a hint of stubble on his brown shaved head, and the line of his black mustache looked like it had been made with a ruler. He towered over the two women and reminded Molly of a rottweiler with his big chest and pronounced brows. In the beginning Richard had Molly wondering if he was even capable of smiling. Turned out he was. By day four Victoria and Molly discovered that Richard was a big softy under his stern exterior—and he had a seriously infectious giggle that could crack them all up.

As different as they were, the three got along well and helped one another whenever they could. No matter how the Sterling Center experience turned out with the dogs, Molly felt like she'd be leaving with lifelong human friends.

When the breakfast dishes were done, the handlers went back to their rooms to get their things. "Pray for dogs today!" Victoria called, holding up crossed fingers.

Richard let out a squeaky laugh. Molly held up her own crossed fingers. She prayed for dogs every day!

In the classroom, Pedro was waiting. He had a sly smile on his face as he began passing out gear. "These are the most essential items needed for training," he said as he handed them each a leash.

Victoria shot Molly a hopeful look. It said, "Dog?"

From his pocket Pedro pulled out three lanyards with whistles attached, clearly to be worn around their necks. He handed them to each of the trainees.

"You can use these to control a dog when they're outside of vocal range."

Next he handed them each two small plastic bags.

"Poop bags?" Richard asked, cocking a bushy eyebrow.

"Keep two of them on you at all times," Pedro said. "I don't care if you have a dog with you or not. I want them on your person. Always."

Molly pressed her lips together. Victoria tapped her foot. The tapping speed increased when Pedro pulled out the last "essential items"—a stack of three white buckets.

"Clip your leashes onto these," Pedro instructed.

Victoria rolled her eyes. These were not the dogs she was looking for.

"I know," Pedro said before Vic could even mumble a word. "You'll get to work with the real thing soon. For now, these are your dogs. Canines will read and interpret your *every* move. It's precisely what dogs have been doing for tens of thousands of years. So we have to make sure that we are sending the right messages. Our attitudes and subtle movements say something. Now is the time to practice saying them right. We'll go through the motions of our commands with these buckets, so when we get to the dogs, you'll know exactly what you're telling them. In the meantime, these lifeless plastic dogs can't get confused." Pedro winked. Victoria snorted, but she did it with a nod. Let the bucket training begin.

🐾 🐾 🐾

Two days later Pedro had a surprise for them. "You've all been doing great, and I think you're ready for your first teacher." He led the trio out to the training grounds where Frances was waiting with Cocoa, her retired chocolate Lab. For a second Molly thought Frances, the founder of the ranch, would be teaching them. It only took a few seconds for it to become clear who was in charge.

Cocoa walked over and sniffed the handlers as if she was inspecting her troops. Her tail was up and her head was high. When she had completed her rounds she sat and stared at them expectantly. She approved.

"You're going to take turns practicing basic commands with Cocoa. She's not as fast as she used to be, but she's still a pro," Pedro said.

"And she's not *that* slow," Frances added. "Are you, girl?" The matriarch of the ranch bent down to pat her partner—the only dog allowed at the center who was neither in training nor currently active.

Pedro shook his head. Frances and Cocoa were both the real deal. Professional. Unflappable. Pedro loved using Cocoa to break in the new handlers, and the wide-headed dog loved showing everyone that she still had the chops. She'd had paws on the ground in more disasters than Pedro could count, and had saved multiple lives as well. Cocoa was a hero.

Victoria was up first and was so happy to be working with a real-life, panting, woofing dog and not a bucket that she got a little flustered. She put Cocoa in a "down stay" and then stepped off with the wrong foot, accidentally releasing her. Cocoa took it easy on the newbie human and gave her a chocolaty stare as she slowly got to her feet. Victoria shook off her fluster, corrected herself, and tried again. They did three more commands and then it was Richard's turn.

Richard was as precise as his mustache, and prouder than a rooster. When Cocoa retrieved the correct scent item from behind a set of blue barrels, he giggled like a two-year-old, sending the entire crew of humans into a fit of laughter.

Molly was last. She was as delighted as the others to be working with a real dog and gave Cocoa a long pat before she started through the list of commands. The big brown dog's soft ears made her realize how much she was missing her own pups. She tried to remind herself that the more successful she was with training, the sooner she would be reunited with them. It didn't help very much. Still, she did well with her commands. She was clear in her stances, if a little hesitant, and Cocoa understood what she was saying.

On the side of the field, Frances squinted one eye. "She's a bit nervous, isn't she?" she asked Pedro.

"Sí." Pedro nodded. "I don't think she's certain she's alpha enough, you know?"

After years of running the center, Frances knew.

Not everyone was a pack leader. Not everyone was cut out to be a SAR canine handler.

🐾 🐾 🐾

That night at dinner—a group meal in the kitchen of the handlers' lodge—Pedro sat beside Molly. When Victoria and Richard were locked in a conversation about dog breeds, Pedro turned in her direction.

"How are you doing without your dogs?" he asked, though it was no secret that Molly was missing them. She'd shown pictures of her BFFs around more than once.

"Pretty well, actually. I'm only looking for them around my legs every half hour instead of every five minutes!"

Pedro chuckled. "Progress!" he agreed. "I'm sure they miss you, too." He leaned in a bit closer. "As for your work with us at Sterling . . . you know that the dog chooses the handler, and not the other way around, yes?" he asked in a low tone.

Molly nodded. She knew the chemistry had to be spot on—and it was no surprise that dogs could pick up on that before humans.

"But sometimes I like to provide a bit of help in that area. Though the final decision is not up to me, I want you to know that I chose you intentionally because I have a very special dog in mind for you to partner with." Pedro smiled a shy smile.

Molly smiled back, surprised and unsure. "You did? Why? I mean, why did you choose me? Or . . . us?"

"I'm going to be honest with you," Pedro said, sitting back in his chair. "I think the two of you have a lot in common: big hearts, a lot of skill, and not a great deal of confidence."

As she listened to the story of Jet—and felt her heart break at his early mistreatment—Molly felt bolstered. It was good to be chosen! She felt inspired to make the poor border collie's life better than it had ever been. Part of her, though, felt even *more* worried. How could she be the right partner for a needy dog if she was lacking confidence herself?

The next week flew by, and all three handlers-in-training became experts in timing commands, playing "victim" for dogs to seek out, mastering a tug-of-war "reward" game, and reading the body language of the already-certified SAR dogs who came back to assist and continue their own training. Before they knew it, it was time to meet the novice dogs that might end up being their partners.

Dog introduction day was a big deal, and Frances, Eloise, Morgan, and Pedro were all there to watch the interactions. Pedro offered advice, but it was Roxanne who would observe and make the decision. She was hands down the best at reading the dogs.

"I feel like I'm on a blind date!" Victoria joked, standing beside Molly in the shade of an oak on the edge of the field. She'd spiked her short hair up for the occasion and looked a little like an Akita with a haircut.

Richard stood on Molly's other side, and Molly found herself wishing he would bust out his silly giggle to break the tension.

She gazed down the path in the distance and saw Roxanne, at last, walking with three dogs. When they got to the edge of the training grounds Roxanne stopped and unclipped them all. The first dog, a German shepherd mix, bounded quickly toward them—fearless and energetic. Free to do what he wanted, he made a big loop, taking in smells before turning quickly and sauntering over to introduce himself to the three new handlers. He was a high-energy mixed breed and seemed to like all three of the partners, and possibly equally.

"Phoenix," Molly read from the smiley pup's tag.

Richard and Victoria both wondered if this could be "the one" for them, but didn't have long to ponder the question before the next dog strutted in. Cadence was a golden retriever. She was beautiful, and she knew it. She worked the field as if it was a runway, stretching her legs and strutting her stuff before stopping in front of Richard to let him admire her. She moved on to Molly, pausing to let her stroke her soft coat before continuing on to offer a few moments of her time to Victoria. Finally she circled back to Richard.

Watching from the stands, Morgan felt as though she could already tell who Cadence had chosen.

Pedro and Roxanne had their heads together and were pointing toward the retriever. Morgan was pretty sure they were thinking the same thing she was, though honestly it was hard for Morgan to think about Cadence or Phoenix with Jet still hanging back.

The black-and-white dog took his time. He waited until Cadence and Phoenix were relaxing in the shade before finally trotting over to check out the new people.

As soon as she spotted Jet, Molly was smitten. His bicolored eyes, his high-flying flag of a tail, his white socks! Of course, she knew that this was the dog Pedro had in mind for her . . . he'd mentioned the breed. And though Jet seemed confident, he wasn't as exuberant as Cadence or Phoenix. He was a little more cautious. Just like Molly. Just like Pedro had said.

Because Pedro had "set them up," Molly expected the border collie to come right to her, and stay. She held out her arms to welcome him, beaming . . . until he walked right past her. Molly stood gaping while he gave Victoria a sniff, plopping down beside her while she rewarded the pup with a full belly rub.

Feeling a wave of panic, Molly looked to Pedro. Pedro appeared calm as he took everything in, though Molly thought she saw a little surprise in his brown eyes, too. Molly's heart sank. She could not make a dog choose her. But . . .

"Oh no!" Morgan whispered. She knew of Pedro's plan and felt for Molly, and Jet . . . and herself. Part of letting dogs choose their people was not getting attached to any specific outcome. But no matter how hard they tried to stick to this ideal, sometimes—like now—they cared too much. Morgan could sense Molly's devastation and remembered Pedro's excitement at having found "the right one" for Jet. She bit her lip . . .

His belly rub complete, Jet stood up and shook. Morgan looked from Jet to Pedro and back to him so quickly her dark twists bounced off her cheeks. Pedro's brow was wrinkling. Jet's tail was drooping. Then, all of a sudden, it was as if the sun came out.

Molly dropped to one knee, her arms still out, but limply, and Jet practically threw himself at her feet. He dropped his head and raised his butt in the air and let Molly scratch him all over. He put his head on the ground and twisted himself into a pretzel while his tongue lolled out. He liked this lady. He liked her smile and her hands and the way she kept calling him "good boy." He liked how she smelled like bread and apples. He liked her chewy-looking shoes and her long hair.

A few feet away, Cadence sat politely for Richard and let him stroke her golden fur. She was a pure princess, and Richard was in love. On the other side, Phoenix seemed to have claimed Victoria as his very own and had toppled her to lick her face.

Roxanne and Pedro came closer. The wrinkle was gone from Pedro's brow. The trainers looked at one another, not needing to speak. The dogs had already done the communicating.

"Well, let's start with this set of combinations." Roxanne clapped her hands once and rubbed them together.

"Looks good to me," Pedro agreed, stealing a glance at Morgan and Frances, who were both smiling widely. Molly and Victoria got back onto their feet, and the three dogs settled in beside their new partners, ready to get to work.

21

The sound of kibble hitting the bowl made Jet wag so hard his whole body moved, even though he was sitting and waiting patiently. Jet loved this time of day. This was the time of day he got breakfast. Every. Single. Morning. He looked around to make sure that the other dogs were where they should be. He liked keeping everydog in line!

Forrest bent down to set the bowl on the floor beside four already-filled dog dishes. Most of them had only kibble, but a couple of the dogs had special diets. *All* the dogs were sitting outside their kennels waiting patiently.

"Okay, eat!" Forrest called, and the dogs

simultaneously dove for their bowls. Jet, surprisingly, was the last to get to his, and he nosed it before taking his first bite. It had taken him over three months, but he was finally learning to enjoy his food. He no longer wolfed it down so quickly he didn't chew it. Or taste it.

"Way to go slow, Jet," Forrest commented, seeing that he was going to be last to finish. Everyone on the ranch knew that Jet was a speedster in most things, and it was good to see him take his time. When he was finished eating Jet carefully licked the bowl and then walked along in front of the other dogs, making sure they were in an orderly row while they waited for Forrest and Morgan to take them outside.

Forrest smiled. "Thanks for coming to work today, Jet," he said lightly. Jet was the first border collie to come through in a long time, and the first Forrest had worked with. Like any dog with a stressful past, it took time for Jet's real character to emerge. After nearly four months on the ranch, his border collie nature was in full view, and his herding instincts were more apparent every day!

"It's like the moment he put the trauma of being tortured and tied behind him, his true personality came out," Morgan said, beaming at Jet. "He's definitely more of a leader than a follower now!"

Morgan and Forrest leashed all the dogs and took them out for a short walk. When they returned, Molly was there with Roxanne—she was scheduled for the morning training shift today, and the other handlers would work later this afternoon. Jet trotted up to Molly and greeted her with a lick, then sat down so fast and so close to her he nearly knocked her over!

"He only weighs forty pounds, but with his rocket fuel behind it, it's more like a hundred," Morgan noted with a little bit of pride.

Roxanne had a sterner response. "Slow down, Jet!" Roxanne corrected him, then remembered that doing so wasn't her job anymore—it was Molly's.

Molly didn't notice the head trainer's slip . . . she was too busy feeling caught off balance both literally and in her own mind. Since being paired with Jet, she'd felt off-kilter a lot, and having Jet nearly topple her a few weeks into their training seemed like a metaphor.

It wasn't that the training was going badly. They were getting through the exercises successfully and made a good team in many ways. Still, Molly couldn't shake the feeling that it was mostly because of Jet. Molly herself was having a hard time finding her groove.

As she looked down at the two-tone pup gazing lovingly up at her, she felt a pang of guilt. She missed her dogs so much! Why did she need to have a working dog relationship? Shouldn't Munch and Sasha be enough? Sighing inside, she picked up Jet's lead and headed out to the training grounds with an entourage . . . Pedro, Roxanne, and Eloise. Lately Eloise had been acting as the "victim" for Jet, and the assistant trainer quickly disappeared up the path to hide in an elevated spot. Roxanne knew Jet could climb trees, but she wanted to explore how he did when the victim was in one. Neither Jet nor Molly knew where Eloise would be hiding.

As the group approached the center of the training grounds, they spotted Juniper near the observation trailer. Her hair was messy, with curls escaping her two plaits, and her shoulders were uncharacteristically slumped.

"Where are your cats-in-training?" Pedro called with a small smile.

Juniper scowled at the posse of adults. "Having a time-out in my room," she huffed. "They both need some time to think about their behavior."

As she said this Forrest and Morgan came up the path. Their pavilion chores were finished, and they had a minute to watch the training session. "If you're talking about your cats, I don't think they're doing much thinking," Forrest said. "Shelby just told me Twig jumped out the window."

"Whaaaa?" Juniper sputtered, her eyes widening. "But my room is on the second floor!" She let out a little shriek and sprinted toward the house. The others watched her go, their amused expressions flooding their faces. Even Molly let out a laugh.

"That one's a character. And one hundred percent cat," Pedro said.

"Maybe a hundred and ten percent," Morgan added with a wry smile as she moved toward the observation trailer. She was not worried about Twig. Cats landed on their feet. And so did her little sister.

Forrest followed Morgan, and they both stepped inside the trailer with its large glass window, modified so people could watch dog-training exercises without being a distraction or interfering with the training itself. In the few times she'd been able to watch Molly and Jet together, Morgan had noticed Molly's apprehension, and Morgan was hoping, like she did every day, that Molly would find her confidence and really start to shine. It struck her as interesting that the timid woman had been paired with Jet, who'd had such a difficult time finding his own way but seemed to be on the path now. Morgan hoped that Jet would somehow be able to pass his strength and trust onto his handler.

"Okay, it's up to you two," Roxanne told Molly

and Jet. "It's a little breezy, but Jet is ready for this." She smiled at Molly, and she and Pedro stepped to the edge of the training area to let both handler and dog know they were on their own. Completing the "find" was up to them.

"Sit, Jet," Molly instructed. The dog did as he was asked and gazed up at Molly. Making eye contact was nooooo problem for him now. They were not working with a scent article—Jet knew what he was looking for . . . the lady who smelled like acorns and chocolate. His nose quivered in the warm, dry air. It was windy today, which always stirred everything up. Catching a whiff of something unusual, he stood and twirled around, as if trying to catch the smell. He felt a tug on his lead.

"Sit, Jet. Stay," Molly told him. Jet sat, but his bottom wiggled on the ground. His haunches were not quite all the way down, either. Molly's brow knit together.

Jet's twitchiness didn't go away when he looked up at Molly. The smells were still a little swirly from the wind, and *she* had a smell, too. A sour one, like worry. He licked her hand to tell her it was okay, but she pulled it away.

"Sit," she repeated. Her voice sounded funny. Jet tried not to squirm. Molly moved away a little bit, and he wiggled closer. "Stay!" she said. She seemed upset. Jet was confused. He was trying so hard!

Molly struggled to center herself but could not seem to focus. She wanted to take time to really connect with Jet before they started, but everyone was waiting for her . . . including Jet himself! So instead of following her own instincts she gave the command she thought he wanted to hear: "Find!"

The word came out like a squeak. Jet hesitated for a half second and then took off in the direction Eloise had gone. Feeling half worried and half relieved, Molly followed. But it didn't take long for it to become clear that Jet wasn't really searching for Eloise. Or if he was, he wasn't picking up her trail. He kept looking around and looking back at Molly. It was like he was still waiting for a command . . . and she still wasn't giving it.

Watching from the sidelines, Roxanne sighed

inwardly while Pedro stroked his beard. This wasn't how they'd wanted this to go.

Jet sniffed the ground, unsure. He thought he was supposed to look for the lady who smelled like acorns and chocolate. He wanted to find something. He wanted to find something that would make Molly call him "good dog." He sniffed his way along the edge of the open training area and suddenly got a whiff of something he loved . . . Ball! Ball made him happy. Ball would make Molly happy, too!

Jet dove into the patch of grass and snatched Ball up in his mouth. Trotting back to Molly, he happily dropped it at her feet. Then he looked up into her face and waited for petting.

Petting didn't come. Molly's face drooped.

The handler-in-training felt a wave of panic. This was not what Jet was supposed to find. And this was not a game! This was a test, and she was failing. She picked up the ball and stuffed it into her pocket. "No, Jet. Find!" She tried to sound confident. Her voice cracked and came out a screech.

Jet sat down almost on top of her feet and barked. He didn't understand what she wanted. Or why she smelled so sour. Or why she had hidden Ball. He wanted Ball! He wanted Molly to play and be happy!

"Arf!" Jet barked. He stood and circled and sat back down. "Arf!" he barked again.

"I think that's the end of that," Roxanne said in her straightforward manner.

"Agreed." Pedro blinked slowly, checking his disappointment. He knew that he and Roxanne were going to need to talk later about what this all meant for Molly, for Jet, and for the team. He hoped it wasn't as bad as he thought it might be. He hoped there would be another chance.

22

Pedro strolled into the handlers' lodge with his cup of coffee and found his human trainees finishing their morning meal at the communal table. Richard and Victoria had started to clear, while Molly sat fiddling with the scrambled eggs on her plate. "Good morning," Pedro greeted them all as he slid onto the bench beside Molly. His gut was telling him it was time for one of the Pedro Pep Talks that Roxanne said he needed to patent. While Molly had all the right skills—a natural way with dogs, excellent instincts, and a strong work ethic— something wasn't working, and Pedro was concerned. Had he made a poor choice? He'd chosen her from among a slew of applicants because of her gentleness, but now he needed her to be firm and clear.

As if coming out of a daze, Molly looked up. "Good morning," she said half-heartedly. She hadn't slept well and was still embarrassed about her inability to manage Jet the day before. And, truth be told, the whole thing was making her miss Sasha and Munch more than ever. She wondered if this whole idea had been a mistake.

"How are you doing?" Pedro asked. He'd learned over the years that it was always good to ask questions and listen well at the beginning of a tricky conversation.

"Not so hot," Molly replied honestly. "I'm mortified about what happened yesterday. I couldn't get Jet to complete a 'find,' or even sit still!"

Pedro took a sip of coffee. "You and Jet have a lot in common, you know. It wasn't very long ago that he felt terrible and was slinking around with his tail between his legs. He couldn't look anyone—even Morgan—in the eye."

Molly turned her attention away from her uneaten

eggs. "Making eye contact isn't my issue," she said wanly. "And you're being very kind, but he's a dog, and I'm a person. I should be able to rise to the task of working with him."

"Hold on a minute." Pedro held up a hand. "Humans struggle, too—maybe even more so than dogs. We tend to think too much." He smiled a little crookedly. "So what's going on with you, Molly? What are you struggling with? Do you have any idea what is holding you back?"

Molly clinked her fork on her plate and sighed. "That's just it. I don't know. I suppose I'm not even entirely sure why I'm here."

Pedro tapped his fingers on the rim of his coffee cup, thinking. "It seems to me you're here because you have skills that you want to put to good use. You know and love dogs, and you want to help people. Those are pretty important reasons if you ask me."

Molly was silent.

Pedro watched her closely for several moments. Finally he set down his cup and turned to her. "Do you suppose it could be fear?" he asked gently.

Molly sighed. She blinked rapidly. She didn't speak.

"Perhaps you are afraid that working with Jet will somehow minimize your love for your other dogs . . ."

Molly felt her chest constricting, squeezing her heart and lungs. She tried to take a breath as tears pooled in her eyes and threatened to spill down her cheeks. She hadn't been able to verbalize what was bothering her, but as soon as she heard the words come out of Pedro's mouth, she realized that was exactly it. She felt guilty. She was afraid that working with Jet—loving a new dog and making him a work partner—would hurt the sweet little pack she already had and loved. She was afraid of betraying Sasha and Munch.

Pedro nodded, understanding her reaction even though she didn't speak. She didn't have to. "I can see why that would be a worry. You love your dogs. You don't want to risk what you have with them."

"Exactly!" Molly blurted tearfully. "I mean, what am I even doing here without them? I'm never without them!" Molly dug in her pockets for a tissue.

"I understand your fear, but I don't think you have to be afraid. You are a dog person, Molly. You already know that love expands . . . especially dog love. Partnering with a working dog doesn't mean you love your other dogs any less. A working relationship with a dog has different parameters. It's rich and fulfilling and will add to your life. What it won't do is take anything away from Munch and Sasha."

Molly gave up on the tissue and picked up a napkin to dab her eyes and dry her cheeks. She felt at once exhausted and relieved, like she'd been carrying a heavy load and had finally set it down. Somehow, in spite of her fear, she knew Pedro was right. The boundless love and devotion dogs gave to humans was precisely why she adored them. It was what made dog-and-human relationships what they were. She sniffled, smiling at Pedro through her misty eyes.

Pedro was thinking about Dusty, the tiny

Chihuahua who recently left the ranch with his human partner, Luis. That little guy had wormed his way into Pedro's heart in a single week. He weighed less than a Thanksgiving turkey, but the hole he left behind was as big as the canine pavilion! "We love our animals with everything we have, but I promise you, working with Jet won't take an ounce of love away from your other dogs. Love expands," he repeated.

Pedro drained his coffee mug and let his words sink in. He could see Molly's demeanor shifting, but it wasn't always easy to take what you knew in your heart and get it into your head. It wasn't easy to change behavior.

"There's one more thing I want to say, and that is that Jet is *not* too much dog for you."

Molly's eyes widened, and she briefly wondered if the man sitting next to her was a mind reader. He'd just put his finger on the other worry squirming around in her mind.

"He's an intense dog, and herding is in his blood. But he's still a dog, and you are his handler. It's your job to make him feel safe and to keep him in line. He could feel your hesitation yesterday. I think that's what confused him. You need to be firm and clear." Pedro was walking his own line now—the one between empathy and directness. It had taken a long time to train the fear and mistrust out of Jet, and the dog needed to move forward with a strong human partner. And besides, after years of training humans, he'd learned that coddling clients rarely produced a good outcome. It was best to be kind *and* direct, usually in equal parts.

"Everyone here can see that you've got the talent and drive," Pedro continued. "But what *we* know doesn't matter—it's what you and Jet know that counts."

Molly used her napkin to wipe her eyes and cheeks again. It was all so much! But she knew Pedro was right. She knew she had it in her . . . somewhere . . . to do this. She just had to dig deep and, more importantly, trust. Trust in herself, and trust in Jet.

"I hope you can put yesterday behind you. It

happened, and it's over. Today holds the possibility of a completely different experience . . . one that you get to shape."

Molly felt her resolve strengthening. The eggs on her plate suddenly looked tastier than they had before, and she forked them into her mouth and washed them down with the last of her coffee. She stood. "All right, then," she said. "Let's get to work."

23

Roxanne was an early bird most days, and today she'd been up before the sun. She couldn't stop thinking about Jet and Molly, so an hour before her six a.m. alarm she was already wide-awake. Not that it did her any good. It just gave her more time to worry. She tried to keep her eyes closed and go back to sleep, but it was useless. Finally she gave up, got up, and went to the pavilion. While she fed and walked and watered, she pondered Molly and Jet.

The display yesterday had been more than disheartening—it felt as if everything was falling apart. Roxanne hoped it wasn't the end of the road for the promising dog or handler.

At eight a.m. Molly strode into the pavilion wearing a huge smile. "Good morning!" she chirped.

Roxanne returned the greeting, surprised to see the handler-in-training looking so chipper. "Morning!"

"And good morning to *you*!" Molly made a beeline for Jet, who lapped up her good mood like a tasty spill. Roxanne watched the two together. Gone were yesterday's desperation and doubts. This morning the pair had the hallmarks of a stellar team, the same promise she'd seen when they were first introduced. Roxanne hoped it wouldn't disappear when they started running exercises. She studied them while Molly clipped on a lead and headed for the door.

Jet was feeling Molly's enthusiasm, and true to his border collie nature, he began to herd Molly outside. Roxanne froze. That wasn't good—Molly was supposed to be in charge, not Jet. The bubble of hope in her chest felt as though it might burst.

Without missing a beat, Molly looked at Jet and made the correction. "No, Jet," she told him firmly.

Jet stopped. His head came up and he walked at attention by Molly's side. "I'm your handler . . . not a sheep. You don't herd me," Molly explained as she opened the door. But Jet already understood. He got it from her voice. Her posture. Her confidence. They left no room for questioning.

Pedro was coming into the large building as Molly and Jet were headed out, and he stepped aside to let them through. He looked at the passing team, and then at Roxanne. There was a question in his eyes, and an answer in hers. "Yep," her look told him. "Things have definitely changed."

By the time all three teams and the Sterling training staff had gathered on the field after lunch, Roxanne's mood had gone from worried to excited. She couldn't wait to see if Molly's confidence and clear communication with Jet would hold under pressure. After a quick discussion, she and Pedro had decided to take a brief step backward and focus on agility before searching. Jet exceled in agility with his natural dexterity and speed but was so good that he sometimes got bored and acted out.

"Let's go, Jet," Molly encouraged her partner softly. The dogs and their people took turns running through the course laid out on the training ground. It included a ladder raised up on blocks, a long tunnel of tires, and a seesaw. The dogs had to stop at the point of balance on the long, narrow board; shift their weight so the board would go down; and walk on. It was intended to help them practice balancing on unstable ground. Jet ran through the course like a pro the first and second times. On the third, though, he was starting to tire of the drill. When he got to the tunnel he ran right past it without going through.

Roxanne sucked in her breath. Beside her, Pedro was calm. They both waited for Molly's reaction.

Molly had been waiting for this, too. She acted quickly—before a swirl of worry and doubt could form. "Jet!" she recalled the dog, who turned on a dime and ran straight back to her. She repeated the command, the one he'd ignored, and Jet repeated the entire course without missing a thing. He raced across the ladder like a gymnast. He zipped through the tunnel. He tipped the seesaw and reported to Molly with his bicolored eyes sparkling. He knew what she'd wanted him to do, and he'd done it!

"Good boy." Molly knelt down and heaped on the praise.

Pedro and Roxanne exchanged a discreet high five. They both knew there was still work to do, but they were all on the same track now, and it felt like the right one.

The morning continued to go well, so well that after lunch Pedro and Roxanne decided to revisit the tracking search they'd originally planned.

"Our victim is already hidden," Roxanne announced to the handlers. She'd sent Eloise out to "get lost" while the handlers ate sandwiches and the dogs rested. "Molly? Jet? You two up for this?"

Molly's heart hammered in her chest, mostly from excitement. She looked at Jet, who was staring expectantly up at her. The answer was definitely yes.

With a quick nod at Roxanne, Molly knelt down beside her dog. She could feel a tiny niggling bit of doubt but ignored it. She had to be sure of herself. She had to be confident and in charge.

She gave Jet a quick scratch behind the ears, then looked him in the eyes, her expression serious. It was all she needed to do. Jet sat up straighter, his ears on alert. He was ready. Molly led him first to the scent pad Eloise had made by wiping her feet in one spot. Jet breathed it in with Molly squatting beside him.

Molly stood. "Sit," she told Jet. He sat. She clipped off his lead. He squirmed, just a little. Molly lifted her chin a fraction of an inch, and Jet settled, giving her 100 percent of his attention. Molly could feel and see how ready Jet was. Finally she gave the command. "Find!"

Jet heard the word and raced toward the canine pavilion, certain of the trail he wanted to follow. Molly hurried after him, trying to keep Jet in her line of sight. Behind her, Pedro and Roxanne followed more slowly, observing the team from a distance. Jet raced past the pavilion, undistracted by the smells of food and the barks of other dogs.

He veered off the maintained trails into a grove of trees. He stopped, lifted his nose, and checked the trail. The scent of Eloise was in the air. It was moving with the breeze. It was on the ground, too. Jet could smell where she'd stepped. Here. Here. Not here. There. He followed his quivering nose.

Molly jogged up to the densely wooded area and paused. She couldn't see Jet anymore, but this was the spot where he'd entered the forest. She felt a bit taken aback. They'd never tracked this far, and she wasn't used to having Jet out of her sight. She ran a short way into the woods and spotted her good dog. Jet was paused in his quest, looking back for assurance . . . assurance Molly was happy to provide. "Find," she repeated, and Jet was gone.

The black-and-white dog zipped through the trees, ignoring all the smells (so many smells!) except for the scent of the person he needed to find: Eloise.

Glancing up at the disappearing blue sky, Molly followed as best she could. She couldn't see Jet, but for a while she could hear him. Then even the sound of him was gone. The only thing she could do was wait for his signal.

Jet bounded through the dense growth like a rabbit, gracefully leaping over fallen logs and weaving through the manzanita scrub. He was aware that Molly wasn't following anymore—he couldn't hear her footsteps. But he knew she was waiting and would be there when he needed her.

Standing still, Molly listened as intently as she could. She heard squirrels and jays. She heard the soft snap of a twig beneath her own foot. In the stillness she felt worry begin to grow, and she quickly crushed it. And then, after what seemed an eternity, she heard the sound she'd been waiting for.

"Arf! Arf! Arf!" Jet barked his alert.

Moving on just two legs, it took a bit of time to get to Jet. At last Molly burst through the brush, ready to celebrate. She stopped when she saw Jet. He was seated in a clearing, barking, but there was no one in sight. She looked around for Eloise while Jet barked again, anxious for Molly to see his good work. Finally Molly followed Jet's gaze . . . up! Eloise laughed when Molly finally spotted her sitting on a branch in an oak tree ten feet off the ground. She gave a small wave. "He got me!"

"Great job, Jet!" Molly said. She laughed, too, and signaled for Eloise to go ahead and toss down the reward she had in her pocket.

Jet wagged and circled Molly, catching the tossed item in midair. It was his favorite reward. Ball! And the happy feeling coming from Molly was pretty great, too.

24

Jet woke from a deep sleep, blinking. He sensed something different. The air was electric. He sniffed. He hoped to catch the bread-like scent of Molly. He wanted to lean against her leg. He wanted to "find" for her. And play Ball with her. And sit next to her. In just a short time she had become his favorite, favorite person.

Since he'd arrived on the ranch, Jet had met many favorite people! But Molly—once she'd stopped smelling anxious and her eyebrows had stopped pushing down on her eyes—was the person Jet wanted to be with all the time. She gave him a feeling unlike anything he'd ever experienced, a feeling that nobody would hurt him, and that the world was a soft place with comfy beds and endless kibble and running and fetching. Molly made Jet feel safe. Safe forever.

Though he could not smell her . . . yet . . . Jet stood up and stretched. He could sense when Molly was coming closer. He started to wag. Molly was coming closer *right now*! A moment later Molly's apple-and-bread smell filled Jet's short snout, his tail picked up speed, and Molly opened the door and came into the pavilion.

"Big day for us, buddy," she said, stepping up to Jet's kennel. She spoke softly. The other dogs stirred and resettled on their dog beds while Molly opened Jet's gate. He danced a doggy greeting all around her feet, and Molly bent down to bury her hands in his fur and press her forehead to his.

When she stood up Jet sat at her feet. Ready. The electric feeling was still there. And Molly smelled anxious, but not sour nervous, more tangy excited. "I can't wait for you to meet Munch and Sasha!" she said.

Jet had heard those words before. Many times. Molly liked to say them and she held them in her mouth like good chew toys, savoring them. *Munch and Sasha.* "But first we have to go out there and show them what we've got," Molly said. "You ready?"

"Arf!" Jet was ready for anything.

Molly clipped on Jet's lead without thinking about it. If Morgan and Pedro hadn't told her about Jet's leash fears, she never would have guessed that he'd been frightened of being tied up. The same went for eye contact. Jet tried to catch her eye as often as she tried to catch his. And when they did connect, each of them saw right inside the other. They barely needed words at all!

"We've both conquered our fears, I'd say." Molly scratched Jet under the chin, one of his favorite spots, and then led him outside. The sky was still lightening, but Molly wanted to go on a good walk before today's ceremony. The demonstration was going to be a piece of cake for Jet. He was so fast mentally and on his feet that Molly could barely remember the last time she'd had to correct him. Still, as Pedro reminded her, it was important to remain consistent. The dog-and-handler team had a lot of training still ahead.

Even after Molly took Jet home to live with her and her other dogs, they would have to keep working and learning together. Search and rescue life was a constant journey. There would always be new things for them to study and practice. "Wait until you see it, Jet. There are trees bigger than these. And flowers and rocks and chipmunks . . . Oh! And snow!" Molly lived in snow country, and as far as she knew, Jet had never even *seen* snow. For a split second Molly's worries started to trickle in. What if Jet hated snow? What if Jet hated Sasha and Munch? What if Jet hated leaving the ranch?

"We won't worry about that now," Molly said aloud when she saw Jet pause and look back at her. She could have sworn he winked.

🐾 🐾 🐾

Before lunch, the Sterling staff and family gathered at the training grounds. Morgan sat up tall in the bleachers beside the training area set up for agility demonstrations. She had to stop herself from running onto the grass and doing a couple of cartwheels to celebrate. She was practically bursting with pride, and the time not so long ago when she feared Jet would not be allowed to train as a SAR dog seemed like a distant memory.

"Oh, be quiet," Forrest said, taking a seat beside his sister and nudging Morgan with his shoulder.

"I didn't say anything!" Morgan protested.

"You didn't have to. I can hear your bragging about what a great job *you* did with your mouth closed." He grinned, and Morgan grinned back. "Jet couldn't have done it without you, you know," he added quietly.

"I *do* know!" Morgan said, acting offended and looking into the distance. Then she laughed. She could never act all full of herself for long—it wasn't her style. "It took all of us. And a whole lot of Molly," she added.

"I love these days!" Pedro tromped up the bleachers to join all four Sterling kids, offering them Takis from the big bag he was munching from. For Pedro, the only thing better than seeing his teams succeed was seeing them succeed while he enjoyed a candy bar or a salty snack! Junk food was not just his weakness; it was his passion. And truth be told he was feeling pretty proud, too. After all, he'd found Molly and matched her with Jet. He'd talked her through her fears. Yes, she had overcome them herself. But he had definitely played a part. Pedro licked an orange-stained finger. He waved down to Molly. She was standing on the field beside Jet, who looked regal in his red vest. Molly waved. Jet wagged. Yes. Pedro reached a hand back into the bag and nodded to himself. Those two were going to do great things.

On the grass Roxanne gave the signal, and Victoria and Phoenix started the demonstration. Roxanne was relaxed and happy as she observed the exuberant shepherd mix. Phoenix had been with them a long time, and she was happy to see him find the perfect teammate in Victoria, who had been smiling almost nonstop since she and Phoenix had been introduced. Their partnership was going to give them both new life!

Molly and Jet waited patiently while the other team was put through their paces. Though there were definitely cheers and hoots from the bleachers for the others, it was clear that Jet and Molly were home field favorites. Roxanne held her applause but felt extremely proud. Jet had come through so much, and had even caught up to Phoenix, who had spent many more months at the training center.

In hindsight, the hurdles that Jet and Molly had gotten over barely seemed like speed bumps. Watching Jet navigate the agility course with ease and bring back scent objects with 100 percent accuracy and zero hesitation was, for Roxanne, like seeing a work of art. She tried not to have favorites—or rather, she always believed that every dog-and-SAR team was her favorite—but when Molly and Jet finished their exercises

Roxanne added her claps and cheers to the mix. She shook the hands of the happy handlers before dropping down to give the four-legged stars of the show a friendly tousle.

The teams didn't have their SAR certification yet, but they were all a giant step closer, and were ready to leave the ranch.

🐾 🐾 🐾

The next morning Molly took her large duffel bag to the welcome center. With Jet beside her in his vest—ready to travel—she had everything she'd come with, and so much more. Inside the ranch's reception building, she was surprised to see not just Martin, her ride to the train, but a whole crowd of Sterlings, and Pedro and Roxanne, too!

"Oh my gosh, you guys!" Happy tears welled up in Molly's eyes.

"Arf!" Jet did a tap dance on the linoleum. He could feel and smell all the emotions in the room and wanted to be up high enough to lick some cheeks as Molly wrapped each human in a hug.

"Thank you!" Molly said over and over. "I'm a hugger," she apologized with a grin and a shrug as she started to embrace the whole crew again.

"And you're part of the family now," Georgia said. Her warm brown eyes glowed as she squeezed Molly back, then held her at arm's length. "We expect you to visit."

"And maybe come for training brushups!" Pedro added.

"Or demos?" Roxanne put in.

Molly nodded and wiped her eyes on the cuff of her shirt. "I'm going to miss this place!" she admitted. "Though maybe not as much as I've been missing my dogs!" Everyone laughed as she looked around the semicircle of people and realized that someone was missing. The shortest someone.

"Where's Juniper?" she asked. "And the kitties?"

Jet cocked his head. Forrest rolled his eyes. Then Shelby explained.

"She's busy writing letters to screen agents for Bud and Twig. She's given up on the search and rescue cat idea. Now she wants them to be movie stars."

"Oh, June Bug." Martin shook his head, smiling at his shoes. "Well, if anyone can do it . . ."

"Juniper can!" the whole crew chorused, with a second chorus of laughter.

25

Jet felt the rumble of the rails beneath the train car as it rolled north. His head rested on Molly's feet, and he sensed her excitement right through her shoes. Every few minutes she reached down to pet him, even though she had her nose buried in a book. Jet liked the train better than a car. There was more room and the movement was more predictable. But he didn't mind cars so much anymore, either. He didn't mind anything as long as he was with Molly.

Outside, the landscape had changed. Instead of buildings there were trees and rivers and mountains. Inside the train car, the smells had changed.

Mingling with the aroma of microwave pizza was the tang of cedar and mountain sage. Jet let his eyes drift closed. He was not sure where they were going, but he was sure it would be a good place. The train car rocked and Jet drifted off to sleep. His paws twitched as he dreamed of chasing Ball.

Molly yawned and stretched. She was stiff from a night of restless sleep in her train seat. She envied Jet his spot on the floor, where he was able to stretch out, or at least change positions! She checked her phone again. They were almost to Seattle, and she wanted to make sure her sister April would be there to meet them and drive them the rest of the way home to the small town of Rockdale. She couldn't wait to sleep in her own bed and, infinitely more pressing, see her pups!

When they arrived in Seattle, Jet got off the train, staying close to Molly's side. The station was large and busy with people moving in all directions. Some carried luggage or dragged boxes on wheels; others squeezed each other into hugs.

Molly was looking around, like she was searching for something. She wasn't asking Jet to find it, though . . .

Jet eyed and sniffed the crowd. So many people. Lots of them stared at him in his vest and showed their teeth in a friendly way. Nobody stopped to pet him. They knew he was a working dog.

Finally Molly found what she'd been searching for and waved her arm in the air. Another woman with yellow hair, like Molly's but shorter, hurried over and threw both arms around Jet's person. She squeezed tight, then unwrapped herself and bent down.

"This must be Jet!" The new woman offered her hand for sniffing. She smelled a little like Molly . . . bready. She ignored the vest and pet him on the head. She acted a little like Molly, too.

The two women fell to talking and Jet followed them out of the station and into the back seat of April's Subaru, where he fell asleep on the padded bench.

Jet awoke to the silence of the engine. It was off!

The car wasn't moving, but outside he could hear muffled barking.

"I'm coming, pups!" Molly crowed. Jet's ears pricked up. He was a pup! And Molly sounded excited! But Molly turned in her seat before she got out. "You stay," she told Jet. "I just need to go say hello first."

Jet watched Molly get out of the car. He pressed up against the window and raised his nose to sniff at the crack left for air. He could smell dogs. Not as many as on the ranch, but more than one. He could hear clicking nails and happy whines and even a few excited barks. He felt a whine forming in his own throat and wished Molly hadn't told him to stay.

Inside the house, Munch and Sasha were showering Molly with puppies love. They had missed their person enormously and had toppled her onto the floor in their exuberance to show her just how much. Never mind that they didn't have a lot of manners to start, whatever training they did have was out the window as they jumped on, over, and around Molly in an effort to lick every inch of exposed skin.

"I know, I know!" Molly laughed and rolled around with her dogs. "I missed you, too!" she told them when she could open her mouth without fear of a dog's tongue ending up inside it. Munch, who was mostly pit bull, plopped across Molly's lap as if to keep her from leaving ever again. Sasha, for her part, panted nearby, showing off the speckled purple tongue that came with being mostly chow with a little German shepherd, Lab, and mystery thrown in.

Finally Molly stood up and brushed off some of the dog hair. "Pups, there's somedoggy I want you to meet," she told them in a happy voice. She knew she needed to keep it positive. If she displayed any apprehension about the three dogs not getting along, they might pick up on it and think there was something wrong with Jet.

First Molly took Munch and Sasha into their fenced backyard. She wanted to introduce the dogs without their leashes on, but in a place that was secure in case they got spooked. Meanwhile, April got Jet out of the car and brought him to the back door. Molly unclipped his leash and held the screen open wide.

"Just look at these good dogs!" she exclaimed. "These are my favorite dogs." Wagging and curious, the established Sasha and Munch pair came over to greet Jet. Jet stood alert and let them approach from the side and walk behind him to get a sniff. Then he wiggled around so he could do the sniffing.

All three tails were high, and after less than a minute Jet knew these dogs were friendly, and he started wagging. He was happy to be out of the car. He was happy to be with Molly. He was happy to meet these dogs—because if Molly liked these dogs, he liked these dogs. The three furry new friends sniffed and circled and sniffed again. Then Jet dropped into a play bow—he was ready to run! The other dogs knew exactly what he was saying! "Chase me!"

The game was on and it was glorious! Molly and

April got drinks from the kitchen and sat on the back step to watch the dogs tear all around the yard, taking turns being the chaser and the chased. After half an hour Molly rounded them up. Jet, Munch, and Sasha scampered into the small kitchen for food, all wags and lolling tongues. As the dogs chomped down their dinners, standing shoulder to shoulder to shoulder, the last of Molly's fears were banished, and her big question had been answered: The new pack was going to work out just fine!

The thrill of Molly's return and the excitement over the addition of Jet lingered for days. Munch and Sasha didn't want to let Molly out of their sight after her long absence, and Jet loved having a whole pack to keep together. He would stealthily circle his family, making sure they were always in the same room indoors, and not ranging too far when they were outside. Luckily Sasha and Munch didn't mind being herded one bit!

The days passed and Molly's pack settled into a routine that included training sessions two or three times a week. The nights got colder—colder than Jet had ever felt. He loved walking in the moist chilly air and breathing in the evergreen smells of Rockdale after dinner. He also loved curling up with his cozy dog pack at the foot of Molly's bed every night!

One morning Jet woke up, his nose quivering. There was a new scent in the air, and it was unlike anything he'd smelled before. Leaving Munch and Sasha in the big bed they shared, Jet padded over to the door and whimpered softly. There had been a change outside . . . his nose confirmed it! And things sounded different, too. Quieter. Muffled.

Molly slid her feet into slippers and joined Jet by the back door, where he was sniffing the chilly air seeping in through the cracks. Molly could see out the small window high over her dog's head, but Jet had to use his nose. "Oh, Jet!" Molly said, looking out. "Let's see what you make of this!" There was a smile in her voice and Jet whimpered again, begging her to open the door.

The latch clicked and the door swung open. Jet bolted into the cold, cold air and stopped in his tracks. His paws were covered in freezing white fluff, and more fluff was falling from the sky! It was icy. It was wet on his nose and tongue. Jet barked at the sky and Molly stood shivering and laughing in the doorway.

"It's snow, Jet!"

Jet barked again. He ran in a circle. He bit the fluff on the ground. He rolled over on his back and then stood and sent snow flying in all directions. Snow. Snow. Snow! He loved Snow. Snow was the best thing since Ball!

"Looks like you're a snow dog, all right," Molly said, pulling her robe tighter around herself and stepping aside to let Munch and Sasha run out and join the fun. She smiled to herself and made a mental note to call Roxanne. There had been one last question in the trainer's head when Molly had left the ranch: How would Jet do with winter . . . and snow? Snow and icy conditions were something that they couldn't simulate in the low hills of central California, and Molly lived in snow country. She needed Jet to be able to search for people who'd gotten lost skiing or hiking, or gotten caught in unexpected storm conditions—that meant learning to track in freezing weather. Searches that could only be successful if Jet liked snow.

Molly closed the door but kept watching the dogs play through the small window. Jet was skidding and pouncing on snowballs and snapping at flakes, having the time of his life.

Molly rubbed her chilly fingers as a happy warmth spread inside her. Snow was here, and Jet loved it. They could proceed with their snow-tracking training, and if all went well she and Jet could be a certified SAR team before winter was out!

26

"Congratulations!" The phone vibrated with the chorus of Sterling family and staff shouts, and Molly laughingly pulled it away from her ringing ear and pushed the speaker button so Jet could hear, too. She'd intentionally called on a Thursday evening, to catch everyone at dinner together so she could share her big news. Earlier that day she and Jet had gotten their SAR certification!

In the Sterling dining room, Roxanne leaned back in her chair. "That's the best news I've heard all week!" she exclaimed with a satisfied smile.

Hearing the familiar voices, Jet let out several barks of his own, spinning in a little circle of elation. Molly reached out a hand to pet him, half wishing she could see the faces of the Sterling clan but consoling herself with the sound of their cheers.

"That has to be some sort of record," Morgan chirped between bites of pasta. Her whole body felt light with excitement. It wasn't that long ago that she was deeply worried about Jet being able to trust . . . and now he was an official SAR dog—ready to go out on real rescues!

"Well, he's always been fast," Forrest murmured.

"How's he doing in the snow?" Pedro asked.

"He absolutely loves it," Molly replied. "And the training is so different!" Molly took her phone off speaker and filled the people on the other end of the line in on the snow exercise they'd been doing while her dogs tumbled around her legs. "We don't use a rubble pile—we just cover people in snow or hide them in snow banks and send the dogs to find them!"

"That's so bomb," Forrest cried. "I want to do snow training next winter!"

With the phone pressed back against her ear,

Molly could hear Georgia sigh. "We will have to see about that, Forrest," she said. "Winter break might be possible, but I'm not making any promises . . ." Molly could picture the boss-mom's warm eyes and practically see her gathering her pouf of loopy curls into one hand.

"Don't look at me, son," Martin added a moment later. "You know your mother and I make these decisions together."

"Parents," Forrest muttered good-naturedly.

"We're so proud of you both, Molly," came another, older voice. It was Frances. "Becoming SAR certified is a tremendous accomplishment."

Molly swelled with pride at the compliment— from the founder of the Sterling Center, no less. She could barely imagine what it must have taken to create such a place.

"We look forward to more of your successes!" the matriarch finished.

"Thank you so much—all of you," Molly said. Now it was her turn to gush into the phone, and she meant it from the bottom of her heart. After a few minutes all three dogs were looking at her expectantly. "I think I have to hang up so I can make our dinner," she added. "We are celebrating with hamburgers, and the dogs are already drooling even though I haven't even unwrapped the meat!"

The whole clan of Sterlings erupted into laughter, and the three dogs who were tangled around Molly's legs barked excitedly in response.

"Keep in touch, Molly," Pedro said. "We'd always love to hear from you."

"I will, and thanks again," Molly said before clicking off. The dogs raced to the kitchen the moment she set down her phone, eager for their dinner. Twenty minutes later she set their raw patties into their bowls, complete with a steak sauce drizzle, and sat down to her own cooked burger with the works. The happy laughter and well-wishes of the Sterling crew echoed in her head. She looked at Jet licking his bowl clean, then circling Sasha and Munch to make sure they hadn't missed a morsel, either. They had made it. They were certified. They would continue to train to stay on their toes, but now at any moment they could be called to perform exactly what they'd been practicing for so long—their first rescue mission. Molly swallowed her burger bite, feeling suddenly full. When the call came they would be ready.

27

"Mud season," Molly sighed one Sunday morning as she toweled off each of her dogs' paws, and then their necks and bellies. They'd just come in after a romp in the woods, and all three of her doggers had a distinct knack for finding the muddiest, stickiest, ooziest mud each and every time they went outside. It had been a warm end of winter, and though the ground still froze almost every night, the higher-in-the-sky sun and longer days turned the earth to squishy muck during the day. Still, all four of them loved their walks in the woods together, which often doubled as agility and scent training for Jet, and pack conditioning for Molly.

Jet loved the changing smells that marked spring's approach and didn't mind the gloppy wet dirt a bit, though nothing made him as happy as running through and rolling in and playing with snow. It had been sad to watch the cold white blanket disappear from the ground. Even the dirty, thawing piles left by the big plow—which he loved to roll in—had gotten harder and harder to find. That was probably just as well, though, since Molly didn't like him rolling in the filthy stuff once the white was covered in street grime . . . or the fact that he'd taught Sasha and Munch how much fun it was to get cold and wet and dirty all at the same time.

"No, pups!" Molly always called to the pack when they started charging toward a plowed pile, though she understood the temptation. Saying goodbye to the peaceful white of winter was always bittersweet, and trying to spend quality time in the last lingering bits made good dog sense.

Jet stood patiently while Molly wiped off the dirt and mud. His new pack had found a steady routine of play and train and eat and sleep. Jet loved it all.

He loved Sasha and Munch and Molly, the work, and the constancy of his days.

With everyone sufficiently toweled, Molly gave the pups fresh water and made herself a cup of coffee. Settling herself on the sofa, she picked up the newspaper while the dogs got to work on some chew toys. They were all comfortable in their Sunday-morning activities when Molly's phone rang. Checking the number, Molly felt a wave of anticipation. It was Joe, the captain of the SAR team she trained with.

"Hello?"

Jet lifted his head at the sound of Molly's voice. He didn't hear that serious tone very often.

"Molly, it's Joe. We've got a situation and a deployment."

Jet felt Molly stiffen slightly. She held herself rigid and listened for a long time. "A private plane went down on the far side of Mount Baker?" Molly repeated. She paused again, jotting some notes on the edge of the newspaper she'd been reading. "Yes, we can meet you there. I think we can be there in about two and a half hours."

Jet was still watching his human as Molly set the phone down and sat perfectly still on the sofa, thinking. Jet leaned in and licked her hand, and she turned to him and stroked his neck fur. Sasha and Munch were still working on their chew toys.

"This is it, buddy," Molly said as she got to her feet. "Our first deployment." She went to the closet and took out the box of gear she used for training. Jet knew this wasn't a training session, though. Molly was getting ready for something. Something bigger. She pulled an elastic tie off her wrist and swept her blond hair into a sensible ponytail. She got out the big backpack and loaded it with lights, batteries, her GPS, ropes, gloves, water, and emergency blankets. Then she packed several bags of dog kibble for Jet and energy bars and nuts and dried fruit for herself. She put on warm weatherproof pants, boots, and a jacket. Finally she made a quick call to April and asked her to look after Sasha and Munch, then strapped on Jet's vest.

Jet held still while Molly tugged the straps to make sure his vest was snug and secure. It wasn't easy not to squirm. Excitement buzzed through his body. They were going to work!

The drive was long but didn't make Jet feel sick. He sat in the passenger seat looking out the windshield—or sticking his nose to the air crack in the passenger window—almost the entire way. The air was changing and so were the smells. He was way too impatient to sleep! When they pulled into the little trailhead parking lot, the rescue team was already at work. A base camp had been established earlier in the day, and Sean, a seasoned SAR worker with a bushy gray beard, was directing Joe and the other team leaders.

Despite this being her first rescue with a canine partner, Molly had been involved in several SAR deployments before and knew that Sean was the IC, or Incident Commander. He was in charge of the whole rescue, an extremely daunting job. She also knew it was unusual for a ground team, and especially a dog, to be called out this early on a plane-crash rescue. Sean explained that the initial team was having trouble locating the plane from above because parts of the forest were unusually dense, and the downed plane—a private charter—was small. Shortly before the presumed crash, air traffic control received a radio message from the pilot that the plane was having engine trouble. They'd communicated for a few minutes, and then the radio went eerily silent.

The good news was that they didn't think the plane had exploded—a fact that made the possibility of survivors more likely. The bad news was something Jet could smell. A spring storm was approaching and they needed to move quickly . . . and carefully.

"I'm Molly," Molly introduced herself to Sean. "And this is Jet . . ."

Sean nodded at both of them. "Good to have you with us," he said. "It's been tough going out there."

Sean wasted no time giving out assignments, splitting the group into three teams.

"You'll be going out with Hendrik," he said to Molly, pointing to a tall, broad man. Molly felt a sense of relief. She and Jet had trained with Hendrik a couple of times. He was smart, calm, and confident.

He also worked for the local backcountry ski patrol and, like Molly, was a regular SAR volunteer. He knew the terrain well. Hendrik nodded respectfully at Molly but was clearly more focused on Jet.

Jet liked Hendrik and was happy to see him. He stepped right up to the imposing man and gave him a good long sniff. Hendrik had a big voice and smelled like doughnuts and cats.

"Ah, you are smelling my kitties," he said to the pup, leaning down to give him a pet. "They shed like maniacs!" He let out a boisterous laugh, revealing the crinkles around his blue eyes.

Sean handed Hendrik a radio—he'd be the one to communicate on behalf of the team. Jet could tell that Hendrik was as ready to get to work as he was. The sun was still in the sky but had reached its apex hours ago, and the temperature would soon be dropping. It was just above freezing, and Jet could smell that snow was on the way. Usually he'd be panting with excitement, but today he could sense that the storm wasn't welcome.

When the briefing was complete, Molly, Jet, and

Hendrik made their way to the trailhead. Molly adjusted her pack and made sure Jet's vest was snug around his chest. She took off his leash. "Sit," she told him.

Jet sat and held his hindquarters firmly on the ground, which was difficult. He wanted to race up the trail and find the scent. But he had to follow Molly's lead. She was in charge.

"Good sit," Molly said. She made eye contact with him, marveling for the hundredth time at his blue and brown eyes, and held his gaze for a long moment.

Jet looked back at her, barely blinking. There were people out there. They were likely hurt . . . or worse. Time was of the essence. Jet got all this from Molly's eyes while he waited to hear the command. Finally the word came.

"Find!" Molly's voice was calm and sure, and Jet took off down the trail, his nose in overdrive as the first heavy, springtime snowflakes began to fall.

28

The well-marked trail angled upward in a gentle slope for over two miles, flattening out at a wide meadow before continuing to climb even more steeply. The threesome had been instructed to follow the trail for the first four miles, and then branch off if and when Jet picked up a scent. The snow fell steadily as they hiked, and by the time they got to the far side of the first meadow, the terrain was covered in a blanket of white. The cold, wet stuff stuck to Jet's paws, but it wasn't sharp or painful, so he didn't mind. It didn't slow him down, either. Molly and Hendrik were not so lucky.

"Hold up, Jet," Molly called to him as she and

Hendrik paused beside a giant boulder. "We need to put on our traction."

She filled a collapsible silicone camping bowl with drinking water for Jet, then pulled out her micro spikes—rubberized, slip-on shoe attachments with chains and spikes on the bottom that would dig into the icy ground and keep her and Hendrik from slipping.

"Strap-on, all-wheel drive for your feet," Hendrik said as he tested his increased traction out on a patch of ice next to a trickle of a stream that ran through the meadow.

Molly laughed at the accurate and funny description as she pulled off her shell to add another under layer. Shivering in the cold breeze, she quickly put her shell back on and zipped it up to her chin.

"Sometimes I wish I had a fur coat like my dogs," she said wryly.

Hendrik let out a belly laugh as Molly called Jet, who'd been exploring a bit after drinking his fill, back to her side. After a much quicker eye contact than before, she gave the command and she and

Hendrik continued up the trail behind Jet while he started to range.

Jet's nose quivered as he trotted up the path, veering off to investigate anything that caught his attention. The cold and wind and snow were challenging to track in, but the winter of snow training had helped, and he was determined. The farther up the mountain they got, the more Jet began picking up scents not usually found in the forest—smells of smoke and fuel and metal. Even weak and from a distance the smells made his nose twitch—they were unfriendly. Still, he knew it was his job to follow them. He wanted to let out a bark but knew he shouldn't. He was only supposed to do that when he found what they were looking for. He knew he was on the right trail, and Molly could tell, too, just by watching the way he found the scent in the air, or trotted back in an arc whenever he lost it in the swirling wind.

Jet moved closer toward the man-made smells, jagging on and off the trail. The wind was blowing stronger now and kept shifting. He paused, lifting his snow-covered snout and letting a strong gust pass. When he'd gotten another good sniff, he turned back to the humans who were following him and waited for them to come into his line of sight. He was sure that the smells were coming from the east, far away from the trail. It was time to leave the marked path and bushwhack up the side of the mountain.

"He's waiting for us," Molly said, squinting through the falling snow and panting slightly. "He wants us to stay close."

Hendrik nodded, saving his breath by not speaking. He was as acclimated as anyone to the altitude, but they were well above nine thousand feet now, and the cold, thin air lacked oxygen. Besides, the wind squalls carried most of their words away. Jet let them catch all the way up to him and accepted some kibble and water. When he finished drinking, he leaned into Hendrik's smelly pant leg and gave his hand a lick.

"As long as you don't start herding me," Hendrik told him with a smile.

Jet's ears perked up, revealing his excitement, and Molly shook her head knowingly as she swallowed a mouthful of almonds. "He knows what that word means . . . don't tempt him!" she said lightly. Molly wanted to keep their spirits up. Though nobody had said it out loud, it was clear the weather was worsening. The snow was falling thickly and getting heavy, and the wind whipped the air.

Hendrik checked the reading on his GPS and then raised his head to take a careful look around. Satisfied that he had the information needed, he clicked on his radio to call Sean. Sean asked him to hold while he communicated with another team but was ready for the update a few moments later. Hendrik read off their location coordinates, then reported, "Jet is tracking well in difficult conditions. It appears he's found the main scent trail and is now leading us off the maintained route."

"Is it safe to continue?" Sean's voice crackled over the radio. Hendrik paused. It felt relatively safe right this second, but the changing conditions and leaving the trail would make it less so. He glanced at Molly, who wore a steely expression as she gazed off into the gusts of white, pulling a gator up to protect her face. "Yes," Hendrik replied. "Safe enough."

"Proceed, then," Sean said. "I'd like you to check in within the hour. Stick together and be conservative. Stay safe."

Jet could sense Hendrik's fatigue as Hendrik reholstered the hissing black box, so he gave both him and Molly a pair of comforting nuzzles. Part of him wanted to bound through the snow playfully, but it wasn't time for that. They were working. They were searching. They were looking for people in danger . . .

The threesome zigzagged slowly across the mountain, back and forth, picking their way through the forest of thickly trunked, high alpine pine trees. Molly shivered in her damp clothes and wished she'd brought ski goggles . . . it was getting harder to see through the pelting ice. They were moving more slowly now . . . even Jet. Before their report-in hour was up, Hendrik's radio crackled to life. "The storm winds are increasing," Sean's voice warned.

"Tell me something I don't know," Molly mumbled grimly.

"But they should die down within a couple of hours," Sean continued.

Though the news wasn't great, Molly was glad to receive as much information as possible so they could be as mentally and physically prepared as possible. And she was grateful that Sean and other team members were tracking their every move. Being out here without that security net would be terrifying.

Stepping closer to Hendrik, she cocked an ear to listen to more of Sean's report. The storm was coming from the east, and the winds would increase for the next hour or two before dying down as night set in. She reached out a hand to Jet, who had returned to them when they stopped to talk to Sean. She brushed some icy snow off his head and back and shook her gloved hands, wiggling her fingers and listening. And then, in the middle of Sean's next sentence, Hendrik's radio went dead.

29

Jet looked up at Molly, and then Hendrik. Something was wrong. He stifled a whimper as Hendrik fiddled with the black box in his large, gloved hands. Molly's body was hunched forward, and Jet leaned into her legs. His paws were crusted with snow, but that didn't bother him nearly as much as the old but familiar smell of worry oozing out of his handler. It was strong despite the wind and her many layers of clothing.

Molly squeezed her hands into fists inside her gloves, digging her fingernails into her palms to keep her firmly in the physical world. She needed to stay calm. She couldn't let her negative thoughts get the best of her. She could handle this. She'd trained for over a year for this—with and without Jet—and she wasn't alone out here. She had Jet, and Hendrik. Hendrik had been on hundreds of SAR missions in this area. He knew this mountain. He knew snow, and winter.

"I'm not exactly sure what happened," he said, tapping the radio against his palm in a last-ditch effort. It didn't help. "But I suspect the storm is interfering with the signal." He reholstered the radio, his face serious but, Molly noted, not alarmed. He showed no sign of fear.

"We have a decision to make. We can either keep going, or we can turn around and start back to the trailhead." His voice was even and matter of fact, and Molly was glad for it. Part of her certainly wanted to give up, to head back to safety. But a bigger part of her didn't. Jet leaned into her again and let out a whimper. He didn't want to go back, either. He was working and didn't want to stop until he found his target.

Hendrik studied Molly's face through the falling

snow while he waited for her to answer. He was a patient man.

"We should go on," Molly finally said. "Jet has a trail, and there are people out there who need us."

Hendrik nodded in agreement. "That works for me," he said. "Onward we go." He smiled down at her, and though it was clear to both of them that they could find themselves in grave danger at any moment, the smile was sincere.

Bracing herself for several more hours of cold, Molly asked Jet to sit. She crouched so they were on eye level. "I know you're on the right trail, Jet," she told him. "We're just running out of time." And then she gave the command: "Find!"

Jet moved quickly over the thick, fresh snow. The team picked their way over the mountain terrain, and though the trail got farther and farther behind them, Jet seemed sure of the direction. He paused and waited whenever he got too far ahead, and Molly and Hendrik followed behind, the wind and their footsteps making the only sounds.

After what felt like several hours but was actually less than one, Jet trotted out from a thick stand of trees and led the humans up a steep rocky outcropping. As she was cresting the mass of snow-covered granite, Molly's ice-encrusted micro spikes slipped.

"Ooof!" she cried as her legs flew out from under her. Her knee twisted to the side and she landed, hard, on her tailbone. Tears welled into her eyes, and she bit her lower lip to keep from crying out.

Hendrik turned back, and both he and Jet were by her side in moments. The big man planted his feet carefully to avoid slipping himself and helped her stand.

"Can you walk?" he asked, sounding remarkably calm. Molly wondered how he managed to stay so even-keeled all the time. It was a skill she'd like to develop. Leaning on Hendrik's arm, she tried not to grimace as she steadied herself.

"I'm not sure," she replied. The pain in her knee was searing, and the base of her spine throbbed.

Neither compared to the sinking feeling that was overtaking her chest.

"We should have stopped to de-ice our spikes," Hendrik said, sounding a bit guilty. "They can get encrusted. Can you make it over here?" She clutched his arm, and he led her over to a nearby rock. She sat back down, and he lifted each foot and carefully scraped the ice and snow from the metal spikes. Jet watched, whimpering in spite of himself. Hendrik reached out a gloved hand to pet the dog. "It's okay, boy," he said soothingly.

"You should have plenty of traction now," he told her as he planted her feet firmly on the snowy ground.

Molly nodded, bit her lip, and got back on her feet, being careful to bear most of her weight on her right leg. It hurt, but she was upright. She gingerly put a bit of weight on her left foot. Doing so made her knee throb, and she held still for several seconds. Finally she stepped forward. She stumbled a bit and quickly put her weight back on her right. She could walk. She had to walk! She tried again, really planting her left foot, and her knee instantly started to buckle. She quickly reverted to bearing weight on the right.

"It doesn't look good, Molly," Hendrik said. But Molly didn't hear him—she was lost in determination. She stepped forward again, and felt herself start to fall.

30

Acting on instinct, Molly braced herself on Jet's back while Hendrik grabbed for her left elbow. The sinking feeling now completely overshadowed her pain, which she barely felt.

"Whoa there," Hendrik said.

"Yeah," Molly agreed. She swallowed back tears and took a deep breath in an effort to steady herself both physically and mentally. She could bear *some* weight, just not enough to walk normally . . . especially in slippery conditions. Still, it was better than not being able to walk at all.

"If you take my arm and give me some support I think I can do it," she said. It would hurt, she knew.

There was no way around the pain. But she also knew from her EMT experience that making the injury worse was unlikely.

"Are you sure?" Hendrik was watching her face, trying to get a sense of how much pain she was in. "I think we should wrap it and give you an anti-inflammatory." He took off his backpack and dropped it gently on the snow.

Molly wanted to argue that they didn't have time, but she knew he was right. If they could work efficiently, stabilizing her knee would actually save time in the long run. "Yeah, okay," she said.

She hobbled over to the rock, which Hendrik had brushed off, and pulled her pant leg up above her knee. Hendrik gave her some pills from the first aid kit, then located a wide roll of white medical tape.

"It's not Kinesio Tape, but it will definitely help," he said as he cut the first strip. He skillfully applied several long pieces around her knee, as well as above and below the kneecap, making it snug but not so tight it would cut off blood circulation. Jet watched, pressing himself into Molly's right leg. She was grateful for his presence and warmth. When the taping was done, Molly tugged her pant leg back down and stood.

"It's better," she said. "I can walk. But I'm still going to need your arm for support."

Hendrik's expression was the grimmest she'd seen all day, but he nodded his agreement as he repacked the first aid kit and zipped his pack.

The trio moved forward, with Molly leaning on Hendrik's large frame. They progressed more quickly than either of them had expected, but quite a bit slower than before. Molly braced for each step but soon fell into a limping pattern of putting one foot in front of the other.

Hundreds of yards ahead, Jet stopped to wait for the humans again. His instinct was to circle back and nudge them forward—to herd them along—but he couldn't do that and do his work at the same time. And he knew that right now the work was more important . . . even though Molly was hurt.

The pup lifted his head into the wind and sniffed

the air. The gusts were dying down, and the smells of the fuel and smoke and metal filled his snout. Behind that, he could smell something new . . . humans! He stomped his paws impatiently, ignoring the fatigue in his own legs. He was exhausted, but darkness was coming and somewhere not too far away people were in trouble. They were stuck, or hurt, or both.

The memory of being tied up and helpless in the yard flitted through his doggy mind. He was so happy that he wasn't confined or stranded anymore! He had been rescued, and now *he* was the one who could help.

As Molly and Hendrik drew closer, Jet caught another scent coming off Molly. Determination. She wore a brave human face over her mask of pain. She paused long enough to inspect his paws, clearing icy bits from the fur between his pads, and then repeated the command he loved: "Find!"

Jet turned and hurried forward. It was harder to see in the fading light, but the snow had stopped and the wind had almost disappeared. His nose quivered and filled with not just an echo of a scent, but a clear, convincing trail. His tail rose and he felt a burst of energy.

Molly loosened her grip on Hendrik's arm. The pain was subsiding slightly now that the anti-inflammatory was kicking in. She hoped she wasn't too much of a burden and was grateful that if she was, Hendrik didn't show it.

Up ahead, Jet surged onward, ranging farther again now . . . far enough that they lost sight of him. Molly took this as a sign that they were closing in.

"I think we're close," Hendrik said, as if reading her mind. "Can you smell it?"

Molly inhaled through her nose and realized that yes, she could smell smoke and burning metal. It excited and saddened her at the same time . . . They had no idea what they would discover when they found the crash. She bravely considered the possibilities for a moment but was soon interrupted by a clear, insistent bark.

Jet had found the crash site!

31

Molly let go of Hendrik's arm and rushed across the snow, ignoring the searing pain in her knee. Jet's barks echoed against the mountain walls, and she spotted his red vest through the trees. "Good boy, Jet! Good dog," she repeated to herself as she lurched closer. Of course she knew that Jet would find their target. She believed in him, always, and couldn't wait to tell him what a great job he'd done! As she celebrated her partner's victory, however, she was also bracing for what she was about to see.

Stepping into a small cleared area, Molly squinted. She peered in all directions and inhaled sharply. The cold bit her lungs and she swallowed, willing herself to remain calm. The first thing she saw was Jet, sitting tall beside several hunched figures. He stopped barking when Molly and then Hendrik came into view but did not move from his post. The next thing Molly saw was the hulking, shadowy outline of the downed plane. It had lost one of its wings, caught on the trees as it crashed. Even in the dim light, she could see a small trail of smoke still wafting from one of the engines.

Molly limped over to Jet, wrestling a liver treat out of her pocket with her gloves on (there would be time for the ball later), while Hendrik identified their team. "We're here to help," he called. "We're from search and rescue. I'm Hendrik. This is Molly, and the pup is Jet." Hendrik spoke loudly, calmly, and clearly. The huddled figures were definitely in shock and had no doubt sustained injuries, but it was hard to tell what was going on. They were buried under whatever clothing and blankets they'd been able to pull from the wreckage in an attempt to stay warm, and appeared like a lumpy pile.

When she got closer, Molly was able to discern two people in the heap. They were seated on the snowy ground, half leaning against a wide tree trunk. A short distance away a third person, a body, lay covered on the ground.

"The pilot didn't make it," a man said, his voice shaky.

"And . . ." The woman curled beside him struggled to speak. "I don't know if . . ."

Molly and Jet both stepped closer to the couple as the woman loosened her arms to reveal a small child. He was limp. His eyes were closed. Molly could not tell if he was breathing.

"I don't know if he's . . ." The woman sobbed, unable to voice her worst fear.

"Stay calm," Molly instructed. "We're here to help," she repeated. She knelt down on her good knee to get a closer look. Jet pushed in close, too, and the mother of the unconscious child pulled back. Her red, tear-streaked face was slack with shock and fear, her eyes dazed.

"It's okay. Let's just see," Molly reassured her. "Jet here is trained to be gentle. He's part of the team."

Jet put his nose to the child's small chest and nuzzled it. The small boy was cold despite being wrapped in many layers.

"We were afraid to stay in the plane. We thought it might explode," the man explained. "But my son has been unconscious. And it's freezing." The man's eyes also had the vacant, haunted look of someone in shock. His voice drifted off.

Hendrik, who had walked the short distance to the plane to check for others, reappeared by Molly's side as she and Jet bent over the boy. "Radio's blown," he whispered. "These are the only survivors."

Molly nodded almost imperceptibly. She didn't want the family to panic. They were dealing with enough trauma.

Molly removed her gloves and pressed her fingers to the child's neck, feeling for a pulse. Jet felt the faint signs of life first. With his sensitive ears he could hear the boy's weak heartbeat. He felt his shallow breath on his nose. The weakened pulse reached Molly's fingers and she sighed in relief. Jet gave a slow wag. "He's alive," she said, closing his mother's arms back around the child. "For now that's all that matters." They would check for other injuries when they'd moved the family to safety . . . if they were able to move them to safety. Molly had no idea how they would proceed without a working radio.

Hendrik pulled a blanket out of his pack and covered the mother and child, replacing their wet layers. Jet stretched across the woman's legs, close to the boy to warm them both as much as he could. His body was still warm with exertion.

Molly and Hendrik quickly assessed if either of the adult passengers had injuries that were immediately life threatening—they didn't—then stepped away to talk about next steps. "Our GPS trackers are still working, I think." Hendrik looked at the small device. The signals it used were stronger than the radio signals. "And that would mean that Sean knows where we are."

"So if he sees us staying in the same place long enough, he'll send help," Molly concluded. That would take a while, though. And she didn't think they had much time. The boy was clinging to life, and darkness was setting in in earnest. She wished she'd packed a flare gun. A flare would have been visible for miles. She just hadn't imagined a scenario quite like this.

Suddenly the radio crackled to life. "IC to Hendrik, come in, come in."

Molly's knees nearly buckled, this time in relief. She'd never been happier to hear someone's voice over the airwaves!

Hendrik must have been right . . . The storm had messed with the signal, but now that the weather was improving it was back, and just in time. The family needed medical attention as soon as possible.

"They're sending help," Molly told the family while Hendrik confirmed that their team had located the crash site.

"A helicopter is being dispatched as we speak,"

Sean radioed. "Thank goodness you guys made it through. Thank goodness you found them."

Molly reached down and gave her hero dog a pat. "Yes," she said quietly. "Thank goodness, and thank Jet."

32

Hendrik and Molly joined the family under the branches of the tree, all of them huddling together for warmth as they waited for the helicopter. Molly resisted checking the boy's pulse too frequently, since unwrapping him meant exposure to cold. When she did check, his pulse was still there, if slightly weaker. She said nothing. Worry weighed heavily over them in the dark silence. The clouds had cleared, which lowered the temperature further. Molly could see stars twinkling above them.

"I'm Hannah," the woman whispered in the stillness. "And this is Sawyer." She hugged the small boy in her arms a little tighter.

"And I'm Nico," the child's father said. Hannah fell silent again, and Nico told Molly and Hendrik that they were from California. "We drove up to Seattle from Sacramento and couldn't resist the sightseeing flight. These mountains are beautiful." He gazed into the distance, his voice trailing off.

Silence fell over them again. The mountains were indeed beautiful, and also dangerous.

"It won't be long now," Hendrik said as the conversation petered out. He offered the last of his Snickers bar and then passed his water bottle around. The chopper would arrive soon, but they still needed to gather whatever strength they could. They weren't out of the woods yet.

"Thank you," Nico said after taking a swig.

Jet kept his nose pressed against the lump of boy. Once or twice the child twitched. Jet knew that was a good sign.

The poor dog was exhausted. With his zigzag tracking he'd probably covered four times the ground that Hendrik and Molly had. Maybe more. He wouldn't let himself sleep, though. He held himself alert, ears pricked up, and was first to hear the helicopter. Only then did he raise his head from Sawyer's chest.

"Is that the helicopter?" Molly asked when Jet stirred. A second later she knew for sure. The sound got louder and soon snow from the ground was whipping around them violently. Bright lights pierced the near-complete darkness.

Hendrik waved his arms. Then he and Molly helped Nico and Hannah to their feet and farther into the tree cover so the mechanical bird could land.

The noisy chopper blades drowned out all noise, even Jet's welcoming barks. As soon as the helicopter touched down, Jet circled behind the people, rounding them up and herding them to safety. Molly limped beside Nico. Hendrik walked next to Hannah, who was still cradling Sawyer in her arms. When they were just twenty feet from the safety of the craft, Hannah stopped in her tracks.

Jet barked, urging her forward.

Hannah lurched. There was panic in her eyes.

She looked like a scared lamb, about to bolt. "I can't!" she shrieked over the din. "It's not safe! I can't go up in the air again . . . we might crash!" She turned to flee, but Jet was there in an instant, gently forcing her back toward Molly, who was reaching out with both hands.

"Our pilot is an expert," she said, speaking close to Hannah's ear so she could hear over the engines and spinning blades. "He's here to take you and your family to safety. We have to go now. For your son." When she finished speaking Molly pulled away slightly and fixed Hannah with a look . . . a look that said, "Trust me."

Hannah blinked tears. Fear was plain on her face, and in her scent. Jet, ever so gently, nudged her forward. Hannah resisted for one more second and then let herself be propelled toward the helicopter door and helped inside.

A few minutes later Nico was beside her, the two of them leaning over their baby, and finally the trio of rescuers was on board, too. As the chopper lifted them into the air, Sawyer let out a tiny, kitten-like cry. It was the first sound he'd made since the rescue team arrived. Molly decided to take it as a good sign. Jet did, too, and gave the boy's forehead a quick lick with his warm pink tongue. They were on their way.

33

Georgia Sterling pushed the speaker button on her phone so everyone gathered around the table could hear. Normally she would be the first person to remind everyone that cell phones had no place at the dinner table, but when her phone had rung, she'd glanced down long enough to see who the caller was, and she answered. She had a feeling this was something they'd all like to know.

"Hi, Molly!" Georgia said when she saw they were connected. "We're all here! How are you? How's Jet?"

At the sound of Molly's and Jet's names, the faces

around the table all lit up. Morgan put a hand over her mouth to keep from blurting out her own personal hellos.

"Jet's a hero!" Molly announced. "A real hero!"

The nine people sitting around the square dining table cheered loudly, stomping their feet, clapping, and whooping and hollering.

Morgan jumped up and threw her fist in the air, sending a little bit of salad flying off the fork still clutched in her hand. "Of course he is!" she shouted. Georgia raised a bemused eyebrow and the excited girl scurried over to get the lettuce, still shouting.

"Tell us everything." Roxanne leaned closer to the phone. She wanted to hear all of it!

Eating stopped while Molly related the tale of the plane crash, the snowstorm, the broken radio, an injured knee, and the biggest and best find Jet had ever completed. "He saved a young family!" she cried. "We never would have found them out there without Jet."

Morgan sniffed and wiped away a happy tear with

the back of her hand. Her heart swelled so much it felt like it could burst! All that extra work had been so worth it. Jet saved three people, one a young child!

"You should see him right now," Molly said, chuckling. "He is so proud of himself. He can barely stop wagging, even though he's utterly exhausted!"

"Just like my cats!" Juniper interjected.

"Um, what do your cats save, dust bunnies?" Forrest poked his sister and rolled his eyes. She had to make everything about her and her potty-trained cats!

"Why, the movie industry, of course!" she exclaimed. "They are desperate for feline talent . . ."

Everyone laughed and Morgan sat back in her chair. She crossed her arms over her chest and soaked in the proud looks from her parents and grandma, and even Roxanne and Pedro. She couldn't have stopped grinning even if she'd wanted to!

She had known all along that Jet had what it

took to be a real SAR dog, and a snow rescue dog at that! And now he was. It just proved her theory that no dog, no matter how broken, loses the ability to find love and purpose. Good dog, Jet. Very good dog.

A NOTE FROM
THE AUTHORS

As bona fide dog lovers we jumped at the opportunity to write stories about rescue dogs. Knowing that the project would require extensive research, we excitedly explored websites, books, articles, and anything else that could help us learn about rescue dog training, handler pairing, and the disasters dogs assist with. We found dozens of inspiring stories about real dogs doing what they do best: acting selflessly, loyally, enthusiastically, tirelessly, and heroically to save people in peril. We were won over by these incredible tales of canines and their companions, and inspired by the dedication and hard work so many two- and four-legged creatures undertake in service of others. We also learned that there are many differing theories and methods of dog training.

It can take years of training and discipline to develop dogs' natural gifts into skills that make them both safe and effective helpers in the aftermath of disasters. Dozens of canine search and rescue agencies all over the world do this important work, and while they all share the common goal of creating well-matched and successful dog-and-handler teams, each has its own philosophy and style. There is no single path to becoming a certified search dog. Though we were particularly inspired by the National Disaster Search Dog Foundation, established by Wilma Melville and her Labrador, Murphy, we pulled from several schools of thought regarding both training and searching to create these dog-inspired fictional stories. We hope you enjoy them. Woof!

ABOUT THE AUTHORS

Jane B. Mason and Sarah Hines Stephens are co-authors of several middle-grade novels, including the A Dog and His Girl Mysteries series and the Candy Apple titles *The Sister Switch* and *Snowfall Surprise*. As Sarah Jane they wrote the critically acclaimed *Maiden Voyage: A Titanic Story*. *Ember* and *Dusty* are the first two books in their Rescue Dogs series.